"Can I hold her?"

Simon's voice was whisper soft.

Cat wanted to refuse. He was leaving after Christmas. But maybe because he was leaving, what harm could there be in granting this small request?

As he held the baby, she watched the man melt before her very eyes.

Simon touched Opal's nose. "She's a beauty, yes?"

Cat clenched her jaw. The sight nearly undid her. "Yes."

He looked at her hard. "Cat, I have no idea what to do."

"You're holding her just fine."

"That's not what I mean." He looked as if he'd been torn in two.

"What do you mean?" she whispered.

Simon's gaze bore into hers, searching.

Simon didn't hand her over. "Come with me."

Cat could refuse, but they'd have to finish this conversation eventually. Before he left, anyway. She owed him that much.

Jenna Mindel lives in northwest Michigan with her husband and their three dogs. A 2006 Romance Writers of America RITA® Award finalist, Jenna has answered her heart's call to write inspirational romances set near the Great Lakes.

Books by Jenna Mindel

Love Inspired

Maple Springs

Falling for the Mom-to-Be
A Soldier's Valentine
A Temporary Courtship
An Unexpected Family
Holiday Baby

Big Sky Centennial

His Montana Homecoming

Mending Fences
Season of Dreams
Courting Hope
Season of Redemption
The Deputy's New Family

Holiday Baby

Jenna Mindel

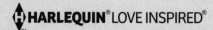

Recycling programs
for this product may
not exist in your area.

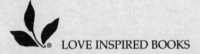

LOVE INSPIRED BOOKS

ISBN-13: 978-1-335-50987-1

Holiday Baby

Copyright © 2018 by Jenna Mindel

www.Harlequin.com

Printed in U.S.A.

In whom we have redemption
through his blood, the forgiveness of sins,
according to the riches of his grace.
—*Ephesians* 1:7

A huge thank-you to Matt and Courtney Font for their insight into emergency room protocol. And to Joan Marshall for sharing a mother's perspective on going to the ER. Your information was incredibly helpful!

Chapter One

Home.

Cat Zelinsky hated coming home.

It wasn't the town. She loved Maple Springs, Michigan. It wasn't her family either; they were great. It was the memories her hometown held. Bad memories of a child who had drowned while in her care when she was a teen. The images haunted her still, maybe now more than ever.

Northern Michigan was one of the most beautiful places even if it held reminders of the ugliest time in her life. It was also a great place to raise a child. She'd never expected to return home with a baby of her own in tow. Glancing in the rearview mirror, she smiled at her nine-week-old daughter bundled in her car seat. "Almost there, Opal."

Midway through her maternity leave, Cat had given notice as a photojournalist for a travel magazine. She'd explored fascinating places all over the world in order to write enticing articles that encouraged the next vacation or bucket-list destination. Not anymore. Those endless, exciting travel days were over.

It had been a long road trip from New York. Cat used to drive it in a day, but with a two-month-old, she'd stopped overnight in Ohio and several times in between to feed or change or simply walk with Opal when she fussed.

"Thanksgiving is pretty special at the Zelinsky house. You'll see." Cat snickered when she realized how much she talked to her baby. She'd started the habit when she found out she was pregnant. After years of counseling, it amazed her how therapeutic simply sharing her thoughts with an infant could be.

Rounding Maple Bay, Cat caught the gorgeous November view that pierced her heart with the warm sense of coming home—followed by the icy reminder of why she'd stayed away except for short visits.

The trees and ground were bare. No snow had yet fallen even though it was plenty cold. The late-afternoon sun peeked out from gray clouds, casting a rosy glow over the landscape, making it look like a painting she might see in a museum. The play of sunlight was fleeting, and in minutes the starkly beautiful vision was gone.

So many things changed in mere moments. Far too many things. Regret didn't help, and neither did self-loathing, but Cat steeped in both. If only she could do things over. If only…

God, help me face this.

Why should He? She didn't deserve God's help.

Cat might have been raised in a Christian home, but she'd been running from God for as long as she could remember. Once she'd realized she was pregnant, she'd asked for protection over her baby. Opal had been born a week late and healthy, but fear that God might still punish her for yet another sin remained a constant companion.

Entering town, Cat craned her neck to look through the naked trees lining Main Street. Her brother Matthew lived only a couple of blocks off Main with his wife, but Cat wasn't sure exactly where. She spotted her oldest brother

Zach's blown-glass shop to the left and a couple of short blocks later, on the right, was the diner her brother Cam ran with his wife. Even Darren had recently married at the end of the summer, but Cat had been too close to her delivery date to attend. All four of her older brothers were now settled down in this resort town. While marriage certainly wasn't in her own plans, Cat hoped she could settle down here too, and that meant finding a job.

By the time she pulled into her parents' driveway, Opal had fallen asleep. Cat took a deep breath before getting out of the car. The last time she'd been home was for Memorial Day weekend. It was then that her family found out about her pregnancy. It had been a strained visit, filled with things she'd regretted. Things said.

Her sister Monica ran down the stone walkway, followed by their mom. Their father brought up the rear at a much more sedate pace, his brow furrowed.

Reluctantly, Cat got out. She fought the urge to jump back in the car and drive away, but there was no place to go. She'd really let her father down this time. Swallowing against the queasiness that stole away everything she'd practiced saying on the way here, Cat took a step forward.

"Wow, look at you! You're a mom." Monica sounded amazed.

"Yeah, look at me." Cat had her doubts about that too. Could she even be a good mom?

She'd never wanted kids because she knew the risks. Cat had not only experienced loss, she'd caused it. Losing a child of her own would be unbearable. Avoiding motherhood altogether seemed safer, and yet she'd let this happen. She had one of her own. All the responsibility, all the danger…and all the humiliation of knowing she'd disappointed her family with her choices. It didn't matter that she was a grown woman of thirty-one—coming home as an unwed mother stung hard.

Monica peeked into the back seat. "Oh, she's beautiful!"

She faced her father. "Hi, Daddy."

"Catherine." He opened his arms.

"I'm so sorry." She walked into them, needing her father's embrace like never before.

She hadn't been sure how he'd welcome her, considering the way they'd left things between them in May. Cat and her father had argued about her decision to raise the child alone, without trying to find Opal's father. Even though her father's embrace felt like a balm, she knew that conversation was bound to resurface, and Cat's opinion hadn't changed.

She'd known Simon Roberts all of four adrenaline-charged days. She didn't believe he was the type who'd want to know they'd made a baby. He was a respected gemologist who traveled all over the world hunting gems. For all she knew, Opal might not be his first, and Cat wasn't about to line up for child support.

Her father tightened his embrace. "God can turn our wrongs into very good things. The best things, if we let Him."

She nearly lost it at the thickness in his voice. She wanted to believe that but knew from experience that some things were too terrible to ever be good.

Simon Roberts slipped into a warm jacket, turned off the volume to his phone before pocketing it and checked his watch. He had plenty of time to arrive at church on foot before services. He'd attended the small congregation for a couple of months now and he regretted that he would be leaving it after Christmas.

He'd traveled all over the world and had been exposed

to practically every sort of religion out there, yet sleepy Maple Springs, Michigan, was where he'd come to know God in a very real sense. It wasn't exactly religion he'd found, although he now attended church regularly. This was something more personal than a list of rules or traditions. It was like nothing he'd ever experienced before.

Trusting God—trusting anyone at all—was new to him.

Over the course of his forty-two years, he'd learned that trusting people led to inevitable betrayal and he was better off keeping to himself. Last year, he suspected that his employer of over twenty years had hired thugs to steal raw opals from him in an attempt to avoid paying him.

After that escape, Simon thought he wanted something else out of life. That was why he'd decided to give settling down a try. Living in a small town was something he'd never experienced before either, and after six months, he'd had enough of the mundane boredom.

He'd picked Maple Springs to set up his jewelry business simply because of Cat Zelinsky. She'd described her hometown as some kind of paradise. He'd given it his best shot, but this *paradise* smothered him with well-meaning folks pulling at him to be part of the community. Simon had never connected well with people and Maple Springs was all about making connections.

Some tricks an old dog struggled to relearn, and trust was one of them. Managing the retail side of a jewelry business was another. Time to cut his losses and move on, back to what he did best—finding gems for wealthy clients.

The community here had welcomed him and his business, but they'd solicited his help with community events and donations. Especially Cat's sister-in-law Ginger. As part of the local chamber of commerce, she'd badgered him to join. He'd given that a go too, attending one of the networking nights, which felt like he'd been dumped into a lake filled with social piranhas. He missed the anonymity that came with living in a big city where no one expected anything out of him.

He'd met Ginger's husband, one of Cat's brothers, at such a gathering. Zach Zelinsky was retired military and a fellow artisan and shop owner who also held disdain for social events.

Simon hadn't properly considered that by moving here he'd meet members of Cat's family. He'd sold an engagement ring to one of her brothers and met one of her sisters when she'd barged into his shop, offering to design his website.

Seeing her family everywhere he went just emphasized the disturbing fact that he couldn't seem to forget Cat no matter how hard he tried. *Catherine Zelinsky* had been on his last gem hunt for Welo opals in order to write about it for a travel magazine. In spite of the danger, she'd loved every minute and told him so when he'd put her on a plane out of there. He'd read her tame article on Ethiopian opals, alongside a bit about vacationing in Kenya.

Perhaps he should have called her, but a mad dash through the highlands of Ethiopia wasn't exactly a firm foundation for a lasting relationship. Not that he understood relationships. He didn't, but it still felt as if they had unfinished business between them. He should have called when he'd moved to Maple Springs, but coward that he was, he didn't follow through.

Part of him wanted to see her again and part of him didn't. She'd touched something deep inside that he'd long ago buried. He'd cast aside need for anyone in his life years ago, when his mother had kicked him out when he was a teenager. He didn't want to need anyone. Need led to pain and bitter disappointment. Any thoughts of a happily-ever-after with Cat Zelinsky were moot. She'd prove no different than anyone else. Eventually.

Still, Cat might visit her parents with the holidays coming, and then what? If she spotted his Roberts Jewelry sign, would she come in or pass right by?

Simon blew out his breath. Nearly a year since they'd met and yet the woman still invaded his thoughts.

He stepped into cold November sunshine and shivered. He'd spent much of his life searching out gems in warmer climates when he wasn't working on jewelry in New York or London. This kind of cold weather wasn't something he was used to and he'd been told this frosty spell was nothing special. Even so, he forced himself to walk the short way from his tidy rental house.

Stepping inside the warm church, he was faced with equally warm smiles from fellow parishioners. Simon nodded and shook a few offered hands but otherwise moved on. He spotted Zach Zelinsky coming toward him and waved.

Zach stalled him by offering a handshake. "Nice morning."

"Bit chilly." Simon slowly drew back his hand when he saw her.

Zach chuckled at his reaction. "This is my sister Catherine. We call her Cat."

She looked softer than he had remembered. Prettier even, with a light dash of cosmetics. He couldn't take his eyes off her.

Cat's blue eyes widened when she recognized him, as well. Her mouth opened and closed before she finally whispered, "How?"

"I moved here."

That clearly shocked her. "Here, to Maple Springs?"

Zach looked confused. "You two know each other?"

"Oh, we've met." The sharp bite in Cat's voice sounded bitter, as if she regretted what had passed between them.

He didn't regret a moment with her.

"We met last December, when she wrote an article about Welo opals. I showed her the mines."

Silence.

Zach looked from Cat to him and then back again, his eyes narrowing. "Opals, huh?"

Simon watched Cat's face pale. Tension crackled in the air and he couldn't quite grasp the reason for it.

"Here you go, Cat. I think she needs changing." Zach's wife appeared from out of nowhere and handed Cat a pink bundle.

"Thanks." Cat shifted the blanket, revealing a baby.

Why was Cat holding a baby?

Simon stared at the bundle, feeling like he'd fallen into a deep mining hole. He looked at Cat before glancing back at the bundle, his innards roiling. Then he glanced at his friend, noticed Zach's balled fists and broke out in a sweat. "What's this about?"

Zach stood rigid, looking every inch the army captain ready to flog him within an inch of his life. He looked back at his sister. "Maybe Cat will finally tell us."

Her white face flushed red.

Simon had no words. Could it be…?

Ginger pulled on her husband's arm. "Come on, Zach. Let them handle this."

"Handle what?" Simon asked, feeling as if that black mining hole was closing in on him.

"Go, Zach. Please, just go." Cat's voice was firm, pleading.

People were beginning to take note of their exchange.

"Fine, but this isn't over." Zach gave him a pointed glare before walking away.

Simon focused on the pink bundle. It moved and he nearly lost his breakfast when he spotted brown eyes like his own peep out from under a frilly knit cap.

"Is…is it mine?" Deep down, he knew it was but hoped for some other explanation.

Cat did not look happy. Not at all. "*It* is a girl. Your daughter, Opal."

Simon backed up a few steps. His ears rang as he stared at a perfectly formed little face. The heat of the building he'd welcomed only a moment ago suffocated him now.

Cat waited for him to say something, anything, but he simply stared.

"She needs changing." Cat shook her head and left.

Helpless, Simon watched her go. He'd always been a careful man, but they'd been under stress and…

They'd made a child.

The reality of what they'd done sank in and it wasn't pleasant. Why hadn't she told him?

He had to get out of there. He could not step into that sanctuary and sit like nothing had happened.

He bolted out the front door and walked blindly until he finally reached a small park that overlooked the brilliant blue waters of Maple Bay. Gulping fresh, cold air, Simon ran his hand through his hair.

He was a father.

"Forgive me, Lord," he whispered. "I didn't know. She never said…"

Why hadn't she called him? Sure, he wasn't cut out for fatherhood—he'd had no example to follow—yet he deserved to know that he had a child.

A daughter who'd need her father.

Simon rubbed his forehead. God knew how messed up Simon had been without one. He also knew how Simon had messed up his brother and sister by trying to step in and be one for them.

His stomach turned. He was leaving at the end of the year. He'd already severed his leases for the house and shop—

Opal.

The image of that little face with big brown eyes flashed through his thoughts. Cat had named their daughter Opal. She was so small and dainty. Helpless. He didn't know what to do with a baby, let alone dealing with Cat.

But the real question was, did he want to stay and find out?

Cat remained in the small room with several rocking chairs for nursing moms. On the other side of the room, two women chatted happily about their babies, but Cat didn't join in. Her thoughts twisted in every direction.

The only reason she'd come to her brother's church was because she knew fewer people at his congregation versus the church where her parents went. She couldn't face scrutiny from all those people who'd known her since childhood as she stood in the same building with the family members whose lives she destroyed. They'd raise their eyebrows at her having a baby and rightly so.

Simon was here.

Cat tried to make sense of him moving to Maple Springs. It didn't make sense. He was a modern-day Indiana Jones—he should be off somewhere having another death-defying adventure. At least he'd made it safely out of Africa and he looked well. In fact, he cleaned up really well and she hated herself for noticing.

Had he given up gem hunting to finally settle down? Her heart beat a little faster.

"You okay?" Ginger stepped into the nursery.

Zach's wife had a magnetic, sunny nature. In the short time she'd been home, Cat witnessed how good Ginger was with her brother. He was not only happy, but seemed at peace.

Cat wouldn't mind if some of that peace rubbed off on her. She shifted Opal. "As well as can be expected, I guess. How's Zach?"

"Oh, he's fuming." Ginger bit her lip, but laughter shone from her eyes. "I'm sure he'll give Simon an earful the next time he sees him. So, like, is he Opal's father?"

"Yes." Cat couldn't see the humor in the situation. "Wait, Simon's not in church?"

"Nope, he left."

Cat had never expected to see him again, let alone *here* in Maple Springs, in a church of all places, but knowing he'd left after their brief confrontation didn't sit well. Not at all.

Glancing at a sleeping Opal, Cat gritted her teeth. He'd left her yet again. So similar to the way he'd brushed her off the morning after they'd stayed in that hut, as if what they'd shared had meant nothing. Evidently, Opal was nothing to him, as well.

Ginger glanced at the other two women, still talking. "He's been coming to church for a couple of months now. Zach invited him. He owns the new jewelry shop in town and makes some gorgeous stuff. Darren bought Bree's engagement ring there."

"I saw it." It was beautiful, a diamond resting in swirls of white gold.

Cat had interviewed Simon last year, yet she remembered that he'd apprenticed under a master bench jeweler in London before becoming a certified gemologist who roamed the world seeking out precious gems. Opening his own jewelry shop might make sense, given his talents and training, but why here?

It wasn't surprising that Simon and her brother were friends. They were both shop owners. Both artisans. Simon had put down roots in her hometown of all places. He knew members of her family, yet it appeared that he'd never admitted to knowing her.

Ginger picked at the edge of the baby blanket. "He's a nice guy, Cat. Too bad he's closing up shop and leaving."

"What?" Her stomach tipped and rolled.

Ginger shrugged. "No one knows why. His store seemed to be doing well, but he's announced that he's closing after the holidays."

Cat might not describe Simon as nice. He was mysterious and guarded. He wouldn't talk about himself and she'd had to dig hard to get any information about his background. He'd been a wealth of information on opals, though he hadn't wanted his name mentioned in the article—only the company for which he worked. He'd said anonymity worked in his favor when buying gems. She'd sent the final draft of her article to his employer and even then no word had come from Simon. Maybe he hadn't even seen it. Or cared to read it.

Ginger gave her a pointed look. "I think he's lonely."

"Simon is one of those men who prefers his own company." Certainly he'd preferred it to hers. But then he'd moved to her hometown, befriended her brother and yet never once tried to contact her. What did it all mean? Was she part of the reason he'd come here, or was it all a complete coincidence? Was she just assuming he'd been thinking about her because she'd been unable to stop thinking about him?

When she'd first met him, introduced by her guide, she'd found him incredibly attractive with his scruffy hair and beard. He had a slight English accent that could melt the hardest of hearts.

Cat's heart had been far from hard, especially when Simon had promised information for an article that was sure to wow her editor. And it did. The article ran a few months ago, right alongside her main piece about Kenya. Those were good days and that was a trip of a lifetime. One she'd probably never be able to take again.

"Cat?"

"What?" She opened her eyes. When had she closed them? She looked down at Opal. The baby slept undisturbed.

Ginger smiled. "I thought I'd lost you there."

"Almost. Tell Zach there's no need to get crazy or anything." Cat stopped, not sure how to explain. She wasn't proud of the choices she'd made that had led to her pregnancy, but she couldn't claim it was Simon's fault. It had been a mutual decision, made when emotions were high and they hadn't been thinking about consequences.

She hadn't written a word in that article about being followed to the point that they'd had to run for fear of real harm. That wouldn't be good for a travel piece. But it had made for a thrilling adventure—one that had left her head spinning, and her good sense tumbling by the wayside.

"What happened? I mean, you know, if you care to share."

The other two women in the room glanced their way as they left and headed back to church. Cat didn't want to go to church. She'd rather hide out here awhile longer. She glanced at her sister-in-law, who was waiting for her to answer, eyes wide.

"I went to Kenya for a travel piece and saw this gorgeous opal in a Nairobi market. It came from the north in Ethiopia. I thought I should check out the opal trade there and my editor agreed. So I flew into the capital city of Addis Ababa and that's where I met Simon, a real live gem hunter. He was able to take me to one of the opal mines."

"Go on."

Cat sat forward. "It's unbelievable how precarious it is. The mines are holes in the sides of sheer mountains. The miners are local folks, and many used to be farmers."

Ginger's eyes were still wide. "Weren't you afraid? All by yourself like that?"

"No." Cat had loved her job, filled with adventurous travel that had kept her far from home and her past. Now it was over. She couldn't leave Opal with just anyone and that had brought her back to Maple Springs and her family.

Cat shrugged. "I always had a reputable guide, so I felt safe. Simon served as my guide to the mines and he has a solid reputation in the industry. One evening, after he'd made a large purchase of raw opals, we were followed. Those men didn't look like they'd play nice either, and the next thing I knew, we were running. We finally lost them, but it was raining so hard we took shelter in an abandoned hut for the night."

Ginger absorbed the tale. "Did those men who were chasing you ever get the opals?"

Cat shrugged. "I don't know. The next day, Simon had a local pilot take me back to the capital."

"And you never saw him again?"

"Not till today."

"Wow." Ginger looked thoughtful.

"Yeah." Cat glanced at the door when she heard a soft knock.

Simon entered, his close-cut hair tousled in the front as if he'd tried to pull it all out. "Cat, we need to have a talk."

Her stomach tipped at the venom in his voice. "I suppose we do."

Ginger stood, giving Simon a pointed look as if warning him to play nice. "I'll check back before church lets out."

Simon held the door for Ginger and then closed it behind her.

He stood slightly taller than average and was slender with a few streaks of silver gleaming in his dark hair. He sat in the seat that Ginger had vacated.

He took a deep breath and let it back out, a cautious expression spread across his face. "You're sure it was me?"

Cat snorted. "Yeah, I'm sure."

"Okay, okay." He raised his hands before rubbing them against the tops of his thighs, clearly nervous. "Have you come home for a bit, then?"

She wasn't giving anything away, even though his nervousness surprised her. He'd shown no fear when they'd been on the run from those men. "I heard that you're leaving."

He leaned back in the chair. "After Christmas, yes."

"Why?"

He shrugged. "Living here wasn't working for me and I'd like to get back to the hunt."

Cat nodded. It was what she'd known all along. A man like Simon would never settle down.

He took a deep breath. "Look, I don't know how to be a good father."

"And I know how to be a mom?"

His eyes narrowed. "You appear to know what you're doing and you've a good family here."

"What's that supposed to mean?"

"You have a solid support system. I will support you too, you know, financially."

Cat sighed. So, they were only a financial obligation to him. "I'm not looking for you to do anything."

Simon shot to his feet and ran his hand through his hair. "I won't abandon my own kid."

He'd abandoned her—setting her on that plane as if he couldn't wait to be rid of her despite the night they'd spent together. She'd thought they'd shared something special, but the morning after proved it obviously hadn't meant anything to him—just as their daughter didn't seem to mean anything to him now…other than money he needed to pay.

She didn't want him complicating things for her or Opal as some absentee parent whose only connection to them was child support. Or worse, popping in and out of their lives. A person couldn't parent halfway and Cat wasn't into taking his money unless Simon showed that he wanted to be a real dad.

"Can I hold her?" His voice was whisper-soft.

Cat wanted to refuse. He was leaving in a month's time. Why bother pretending to care if he wasn't going to make any commitment to stick around? And yet because he was leaving, what harm could there be in granting this small request?

With a sigh, she got up and walked toward him and settled Opal in his arms. She continued to support the baby from underneath and, being this close, she caught the light scent of Simon's spicy cologne. "Cradle her so you don't drop her. Okay, that's it."

"I've held a baby before." He awkwardly adjusted his arms.

"Yeah? When?"

A dark shadow crossed his face. "A long, long time ago."

"Support her neck." Cat finally relinquished her hold and stepped back, curious. "What baby did you hold?"

"My little sister and brother." Simon cradled their daughter and his face softened.

"Ah, so you do have family." He'd refused to answer that question before.

"If you can call them that, yes." Simon didn't elaborate and concentrated on Opal's face.

Cat watched the man melt before her very eyes. The sight nearly undid her.

He looked back up at her. "Cat, I have no idea what to do."

"You're holding her just fine."

"That's not what I mean." He looked as if he'd been torn in two.

"What do you mean?" she whispered.

Simon's gaze bore into hers, searching.

A different woman stepped into the room with a crying infant and her eyes widened when she spotted Simon.

"You'd better go." Cat reached for Opal.

Simon didn't hand her over. "Come with me."

Her stomach flipped again, but Cat killed the butterflies swirling there. "Where?"

"My house isn't far." He waited for her to decide.

Cat could refuse, but they'd have to finish this conversation eventually. Before he left, anyway. She supposed she owed him that much.

Glancing at the woman waiting for Simon to leave so she could feed her baby, Cat quickly grabbed her diaper bag and followed him out.

Chapter Two

Simon held open the door to his rental house for Cat and the baby. She stepped inside and set Opal, bundled inside a car seat, down in a puddle of sun shining on the hardwood floor. She took off the little fleece blanket that covered the baby and looked around.

"Would you care for tea?" Simon walked past her into the kitchen.

Cat shook her head. "Thank you, but no. I shouldn't stay long."

He didn't know why not. He'd faced her lion of a brother in the sanctuary on their way out the door and had told him that Cat was coming home with him so they could figure out a few things. Simon didn't know where to start, so perhaps a tour might break the tension. "Let me show you around. It's not much, but there are two bedrooms."

Room enough for Opal.

What was he thinking? He couldn't care for an infant. One glance at the protective way Cat checked on the baby, and Simon had his doubts about her ever letting the child out of her sight, much less leaving the baby alone with him.

His baby—whom he never would have known about if he hadn't seen her in church today.

Why hadn't she told him?

Cat followed him in icy silence. His place might be small, but it was tidy with a nice-sized wood-burning fireplace in the corner and big windows and a view of Maple Bay. The short hall led to two bedrooms across from each other and a full bath at the end. His room was sparsely furnished with only a bed and nightstand. He'd never felt the need to own more than the essentials.

"There's no pictures or anything. Have you packed things up already?" Cat kept looking around as if she expected more.

"No, this is it." He'd never owned artwork and he certainly didn't have family portraits to hang. He didn't remember his mother taking pictures. But then, she'd never spend money on a camera. Not when drugs had been more important.

Back in the living room, Cat sat on the tan couch. His furnishings might be well made, but he got the feeling they were lacking under her critical gaze. "How long have you been here?" she asked.

He sat in the only other piece of furniture in the room, a handcrafted rocking chair with a curved high back. "I moved here the end of May."

"Why?"

Simon stopped rocking and looked at her. "I guess I wanted a break. The way you described Maple Springs, I thought it'd be the perfect place to design and sell jewelry on a smaller scale."

"Isn't it?"

He shrugged. "It is, but I'm done. I want to get back to what I do best."

"Are you selling the store?"

"I have a lease. It doesn't end until May, but the owner has agreed to let me break it early. I'll liquidate inventory and then move on." That plan didn't feel quite right anymore.

Cat didn't look comfortable, considering the way she perched on the edge of the couch.

"Relax, Cat, we'll work this out." He had no idea what he was talking about, but equally confusing was her anxiety. She had nothing to fear from him.

If anyone should be scared, it was him. For the first time in his life, he'd fathered a child. He wasn't sure how that would change his life but knew it would.

She noticed the Bible on top of his journal and ran her fingers over the top. "And this? I didn't think you were religious before—though I guess we never actually discussed it."

"True. I wasn't interested in faith when we met. But since I've been here, I've found God. I surrendered my life to the Lord in that community church where your brothers attend."

"So, you know Zach pretty well?"

Simon wasn't sure about that, but he'd felt a certain kinship with the man. "Well enough, I suppose."

Opal fussed and Cat stood. "He's not happy about this, you know."

"I can't say I blame him." Simon stood too. "Might I have another go at holding her?"

Cat's pretty blue eyes clouded over. They were the color of star sapphires he'd found in Sri Lanka. Finally, she nodded, picked up the baby and then settled her in his arms as she had before.

Opal quieted, her eyes wide as she gazed up at him.

That baby gaze hit him in the midsection. He ran his

finger down the baby's cheek, knowing he couldn't abandon her.

Simon didn't know much about babies, but Opal struck him as a beautiful one. "You're a pretty miss, aren't you?"

"She favors you, I think." Cat looked as if she hadn't meant to say that.

"No, I'd say she's pretty like her mom." Simon stared at Cat, drinking in the sight of her. In all his imaginings of what he'd say if he saw her again, he'd never expected this. "I don't have a clue where to begin."

Cat forced a smile. "I know."

Opal fussed before letting out a howl that made Simon wince.

Cat gave an awkward laugh. "I've learned to interpret that cry. I was hoping to get home first, but apparently that's not going to happen. Do you mind if I use your, uh, bedroom to feed her?"

Simon felt his face flush. "By all means."

Watching her walk away, he clenched his jaw, remembering the last time she'd walked away, after the intimate night they shouldn't have shared. Why hadn't Cat taken— He halted that rabbit trail. Opal was as much his responsibility, maybe even more so. Cat had been cold and scared, thanks to the rain and the men they'd had to flee. She'd trusted him to keep her safe. Too bad he hadn't kept her safe from him.

He stepped into the kitchen and filled the teakettle with fresh water before placing it over a high heat. Rubbing the back of his neck, he considered all the things that went into caring for a baby. A monumental amount of things. He wasn't ready for that.

He prayed for direction but couldn't grasp that settling of his spirit. The peace he'd recently realized now eluded him once again. Opal was a game changer and he had no idea of the rules or even how to play.

By the time he'd fully steeped his tea bag, Cat came down the hall, carrying a sleeping baby.

"Well, I'd better get going." Cat could not look more beautiful. Her dark blond waves framed her face and wide blue eyes. And his child in her arms just made the picture prettier. He still had so many questions for Cat—about Opal, and about everything that had happened in the past year. They hadn't scratched the surface of anything.

"Why didn't you contact me about Opal? I know I'm not the easiest person to reach, but you could have sent a message to me through my employer."

She settled the sleeping baby back in the car seat and wouldn't look at him. "I don't know, Simon. I…"

"What?" He prodded.

Her gaze met his and he was stunned by the stark emotions he found there. "I didn't really know you." Then she looked away. "I figured you'd rather not know."

So she'd called the shots, without giving him a chance to decide what he wanted. An inadequate answer on every level, especially since it was sheer chance that he'd discovered the truth. Had she come home after the New Year, he'd have been gone without a peep that he'd even been in Maple Springs.

"You figured wrong."

Her blue eyes widened. "Can we talk some other time? I'm really tired."

For the first time, he noticed the faint smudges under her eyes and the fight went out of him. "Another time, then. I think we should exchange numbers, though, just in case."

Cat nodded and gave him her number.

He entered the information in his phone and then gave

her his business card. "That's got the shop hours on it. I'm closed tomorrow. I close Sundays and Mondays."

She slipped the card into the diaper bag but didn't say anything.

This was all wrong, but he didn't know how to make it right. Cat did look weary and he didn't want to be the source of more worry. "Thank you."

She paused before leaving, her brow furrowed. "For what?"

He took a deep breath and calmed down. "For letting me hold her."

Her eyes filled with tears. "Yeah. Sure."

He didn't know if he should try to comfort her or simply let her go. This was all new to him. He'd never been close to a woman before. He'd never wanted more than a temporary or casual relationship. He had to admit that he'd given Cat no indication that he'd care to know about Opal. He'd known there was a chance that their actions could have had consequences, but he'd made no effort to check in with her afterward. Part of him wished he didn't know, since ignorance was bliss and knowing was...

Relationships had always ended, but having a daughter wouldn't. Opal was his and would always be his. The question was, what would he be to her?

He took a step forward. "Need help with the seat?"

"I've got it. No worries." Cat waved him away. She looked plenty worried to him, as if she carried the weight of the world in her arms instead of a wee one.

He watched as she backed up her car and drove away. As he stepped inside his house, it felt far too empty. The hollow sensation in the pit of his belly was unwelcome, as well. He'd lived alone for so long, coming and going as he pleased, he'd never wanted any other way. He'd tried something different by moving to Maple Springs but resisted the community that tried to embrace him. He'd never allowed himself to truly belong.

Now he belonged to someone named Opal. He was her father.

Fathers were supposed to be there for their kids, open to all kinds of disappointments and hurts along the way. Simon had experienced God's love in a tangible way he couldn't begin to explain and was still trying to figure out.

God would not want him to simply walk away, but really, the responsibility was daunting. Could he become a good father by starting out with a young one? Only God knew.

Cat entered her parents' home and leaned against the door after she closed it. Opal still slept in her car seat. Cat wouldn't mind a little sleep too. Forever came to mind, but she was no storybook princess and Simon was no prince ready to kiss her back to life. In fact, he had a nice escape route planned. Again.

Simon.

It hurt that he'd lived in her hometown for months, knew her brothers and yet hadn't made one move to contact *her*. Zach hadn't even known that they knew each other.

"Cat?" Her mom's voice pierced the fog of her thoughts. "You okay, honey?"

She shook her head, horrified at the tears rolling down her cheeks.

Her mom didn't hesitate to wrap her arms around her. "Tell me what happened."

Cat shuddered with a shoulder-shaking sob.

"Andy, come get the baby out of the doorway." Her mom led her into the living room.

"What's wrong with her?" Cat heard her father's whisper.

Then she heard Zach's booming voice. "Is that Cat? Is she crying? I'll kill him!"

"Zach, settle down!" her mother warned and then turned to Cat. "What happened? Is this about Simon? Zach told me. He's Opal's father, isn't he?"

Cat nodded. No point in denying it.

"I knew it! That slimy—" Zach's voice startled Opal awake, so he continued his rant in a whisper. "All this time and he never said a word about you—"

"Zach! That's enough." Their mom's tone broached no argument and her brother zipped it.

Cat's father picked up Opal and walked with her, gently shushing the now-crying babe.

Cat pulled away from her mom. She hated to admit that seeing Simon hurt more than she'd ever expected. "Simon was fine. I'm just tired and my hormones are out of whack."

Zach took a step back as if she'd admitted to having the plague or worse.

Her mom winked. "Come upstairs. You should sleep when you can or you'll go crazy."

Maybe she'd already gone mad. She thought she could do this on her own, but one look at Simon holding their daughter and she wasn't so sure.

It seemed like another lifetime when Simon had wrapped his arms around her, making her feel price-less, like some rare gem he'd searched for his whole life. He'd kissed her that way too, but it had been because of their flight in the night. It hadn't been real; otherwise he would have tried to see her again. He would have at least admitted to her family that he'd met her.

She followed her mom, who'd taken Opal, and headed up the stairs. Once in her old room, Cat sat on the bed and watched as her mom laid Opal in the old crib they'd hauled down from the attic.

"Make sure she's on her back." Her voice sounded too shrill.

"I know, Cat. It's okay. You said Simon was fine with all this?" Her mom's voice was whisper-soft as she wrapped the baby in a swaddling blanket.

"Not quite." He'd looked like she'd put him inside a snow globe and shaken hard.

"Then how was he?" Her mom's shrewd gaze locked onto hers.

"I didn't think I'd ever see him again." It was all Cat could muster.

Her mom nodded. Like so many times growing up when Cat hadn't given up the whole story, her mom simply waited. And like always, Cat crumbled under that steady gaze. "He's leaving after the holidays. But he said he'd give financial support."

"That's good."

"Is it?" Cat couldn't get the image of him holding Opal out of her mind. He'd been captivated, as if he couldn't believe such a treasure existed.

Her mom's gaze narrowed. "The last time you were home, you were adamant about raising Opal on your own. You refused to name the father, let alone contact him."

"I know." The last time she'd been home, Simon had been on his way to moving here. Crazy. She'd been so sure of herself then. Cat didn't know what she wanted now, after seeing him.

Her mom brushed Cat's hair back as if she were still a child. "Sleep now. Things will look better after you wake up."

No, they wouldn't. They'd be the very same.

"Don't worry about dinner. I'll make sure you get a plate." Her mother kissed her forehead.

Cat nodded.

At the door, her mother turned. "Why don't you invite Simon to join us for Thanksgiving?"

Not a good idea. "I don't know his plans."

The sudden thought that he might be seeing someone seared her belly and turned it sour. But surely he wouldn't leave if that was true. And anyway, Ginger would have said something.

Her mom smiled. "Just ask."

"I don't know." Cat lay back on her bed and stared at the ceiling.

"Cat, if Simon wants to be supportive, let him be more than a monthly check."

Did he really want to be part of Opal's life—part of *her* life? Maybe everything he'd done and said today had just been the result of surprise. He might feel differently in the morning. It wouldn't be the first time.

Leaving Simon in the dark about Opal might not have been fair, but if he'd cared about her at all, he would have contacted her. She would have told him about the baby if he had.

There was no way to rewrite the past. She'd have to decide how to handle things going forward. Having him around her whole family was bound to be awkward, but maybe her mom was right. If Simon wanted to be part of Opal's life, it had to start now, not years later. That wouldn't be fair to Opal.

She glanced at the baby lying peacefully in her crib, asleep once again. Her heart twisted at the sweetness of her daughter's face. She reached for her phone and took a quick photo. "You deserve the best, baby. I hope I can give you that."

Every child deserved to know their father. Now that Simon knew, and while he was still here in Maple Springs, she owed him the chance to be part of Opal's life. That meant being involved with the Zelinsky family, as well. Simon knew Zach, he might as well get to know the rest of them.

The next day, Simon watched for Cat. She'd called and asked if they could go for a drive to talk and he'd agreed. When she pulled in, he was already waiting outside and slipped into the passenger seat. "Hello."

"Good morning." Cat looked pretty with her blond hair mostly pulled back with some of it loose.

He glanced in the back seat at Opal and smiled. "Good morning, Princess."

Cat stared at him as if he'd lost his mind.

"What?" he asked.

"Nothing."

"Well, where to?" Simon liked the idea of talking while driving, although he'd rather be the one behind the wheel.

"I need to pick up a few things for Opal in the next town over. Do you mind going with me?"

"They carry good stuff?" Simon asked.

"Yes. Traverse City has more stores, but that's two hours away."

"We don't need to go that far."

He'd been thinking a lot about this situation, coming up with nothing new. All he knew was that it wasn't right to abandon his own child. Paying child support was part of being a father, but would it be enough?

They slipped into silence while Cat drove out of town. Even the baby remained quiet.

"Do you have plans for Thanksgiving?" Cat's voice sounded strained.

"Nothing special. Why?"

"My mother wants you to come to our house for the day." Cat didn't look over at him as she rounded the bay.

Simon fought his instinct to refuse outright and stalled. "What do *you* want?"

"I want you to come. I'd like you to get to know my family."

If the rest of Cat's family reacted as Zach had, he'd rather face a firing line. Still, perhaps that was what he deserved. His actions had consequences. Opal being one of them. Time to take responsibility, even as he searched for a way out. "I don't want to intrude."

"You wouldn't be. They're nice people, Simon."

"I'm sure they are—"

"If you don't have other plans, then what is it?" Cat glanced at him.

He shrugged. "I'm not used to family gatherings."

Cat softened. A little. "What about your family? You mentioned having a brother and sister."

He might as well let her know where he came from. "My brother's in jail for assault the last time I checked and I haven't spoken to my sister in years. Both are much younger than me."

"And your parents?" Cat squeaked out.

"My mom died a few years back and I never knew my father." He kept his voice even.

Cat watched the road a moment longer before stealing another peek at him. "I'm sorry."

He didn't want her sympathy.

She kept going, trying to make conversation. "So, your mother never remarried?"

He laughed and it came out as a harsh-sounding bark. "She never married in the first place. I didn't know my father because I don't know who that man might be. I don't think my mother knew either. My siblings are pretty much in the same boat. Only, they know their father. But he's never wanted anything to do with either of them."

"Oh." Cat looked truly sorry.

"I vowed never to follow those footsteps and yet here I am."

Cat winced. "Yes, here we are."

They'd messed up.

They arrived at the store. Cat pulled into the parking lot but hesitated about getting out. She turned to face him. "Look, I'm sorry this happened."

He didn't like the repentant look on her face.

He'd never meant to slam her like this was all her fault. He reached for the bit of her hair that brushed her shoulders, feeling the silkiness of it between his fingers. "I'm not."

Her eyes widened.

He couldn't believe he'd just said that, but oddly he meant it. He realized that seeing her was better than not. Even though she came with serious baggage that had the same brown eyes as him. "We'll figure it out."

She gave him a hint of a smile. "You keep saying that."

"We don't have much of a choice, now do we?"

She looked away, clearly disappointed. "No, I suppose not."

He couldn't expect to chase away her fears when he had so many of his own. But he'd try. He had to try.

Cat's stomach sank as she got out of the car. She had no right to be disappointed in his answer. Simon was doing his best to deal with their situation. It was not as if he'd had much time to get used to becoming a father. She'd stolen that time from him by not telling him.

He opened the door to the back seat and Opal. "How do I do this?"

She came around and slid the car seat out of its base. "Like that. Super easy. And if you hold her, I'll get the stroller from the trunk."

"Stroller?"

"You'll see." Cat popped the trunk and withdrew the folded stroller. She then snapped the car seat into place. "I'm not real comfortable setting Opal in a shopping cart. The car seat might not fit right and then what if she fell or something fell on her?"

"I see your point." Simon tucked the edge of the blanket that had flopped over around their daughter's shoulders. "Will she be warm enough without a coat?"

The temperatures were still cold, but the sun shone from a cloudless sky. Cat felt her baby's nice warm cheeks against her cold hands. "The blanket keeps her warm. It's not far. If you'll push her, I'll get us a cart."

Simon took over stroller duty. He hadn't shaved and the day-old whiskers roughed his face. He looked like the man she'd met in Africa. Only, he wore jeans and a thick woolen sweater instead of dusty khakis and a sweat-soaked T-shirt.

She looked down at her feet. She didn't match his smooth style wearing her Goth-style clunky black boots, leggings and a long black sweater. They didn't match at all, and that was part of the problem. Despite his promises to figure it out, they were not any closer to a plan or solution to the question of "what now?"

When they entered the store, Cat took in the Christmas decorations with a frown. She hadn't expected Northern Michigan retailers to be in sync with bigger cities. "Thanksgiving's not even over yet."

He nodded. "I need to decorate my store. Part of a holiday liquidation plan."

"I'd like to see it. The engagement ring Darren bought

for Bree is gorgeous." She wanted to see more of his work, especially what he may have done with those raw opals he'd bought while she'd tagged along. He'd said that he'd often been paid with a selection of the gems he'd purchased for his employer.

"Stop by anytime."

They made their way toward the baby section and she took a deep breath. "Here we go."

Simon chuckled. "You look like I feel. I have no idea about these things."

Cat laughed too. "I'm still figuring it out."

He touched her arm, bringing them to a stop.

Cat looked into his warm brown eyes. "What?"

"I'm sorry you were alone."

Cat's belly flipped at the softness of his voice. To keep her thoughts away from what might have been, she tried to focus on the Thanksgiving-themed items shelved in the middle of the wide aisle, but the bagged stuffing and rows of bottled sage spices didn't stave off the swell of emotions that assaulted her. Regret that he hadn't been there.

Her voice came out thick when she answered, "I wasn't alone. My mom was with me when Opal was born."

He ran his hand through his hair, shorter now and much neater. "I should have been there. I would have been there had I known."

"Would you really? You didn't even mention that you'd met me to Zach."

His face reddened. "We both had chances we let pass by."

A safe answer that was no answer at all. What might have happened had she called him when she'd found out she was pregnant? She heard Opal gurgle and peeked into the stroller.

Opal cooed again.

A passerby stopped and smiled. "Awww. She's adorable. Your first?"

Cat nodded.

"Congratulations."

"Thank you," she and Simon answered in unison.

She looked at him.

He looked back, a slight smile tugging at the corners of his mouth. "Come on, we'd better get what you came here for."

And get out quick.

They moved deeper into the store and Cat glanced at Simon. The entire way, his face looked blank and hard, as if it had been carved out of stone. Maybe he was trying not to think about what might have been, as well. Although, she didn't quite believe that he wasn't sorry about this. He wasn't any more comfortable with the idea of being a parent than she.

We don't have much of a choice, now do we?

Those words echoed through her thoughts as they shopped, checked out and loaded the purchases into the trunk of her Honda. Cat showed Simon how Opal's car seat worked, slipping it out of the stroller and back into the base. With the baby safely tucked into the back seat of the car, she showed him how to fold up the stroller.

He looked thoughtful and then took a picture of the car seat with his phone. He'd checked while they were inside, but they didn't carry the same model at this store. "Next time I'm in Traverse City, perhaps I'll purchase one of those."

"What for? You're leaving."

His brow furrowed. "Yes, but I'll be back."

"What's that mean?" Was he planning to just pop in and out of Opal's life? And hers?

"I haven't figured it out yet."

Remembering the rough-and-tumble way Simon drove to the opal mines, the thought of him driving with Opal wasn't welcome. She glanced at the baby. She snoozed peacefully, having fallen asleep while they were checking out.

"What kind of car do you have?" She hadn't seen it in his driveway. But then, it could have been in the garage.

Simon grinned. "A very stable Jeep Cherokee."

Cat nodded. "Next time, you drive."

"So you can see how I do?"

"Yes. Is that so bad? How do I know you won't forget to drive on the right side of the road?"

He laughed. "No, Cat. It's not bad. Actually, it's cute. Now, how about lunch?"

It was noon and Cat was hungry, but sitting across from Simon with so little to say and everything that should be said hanging between them wasn't exactly a prospect she relished. That comment about him coming back had given her a sense of optimism, but Cat knew better than to hope for impossible things. Coming back didn't mean staying. "Where do you want to go?"

He pointed at the three chain restaurants lined up across the street. "How about one of those?"

"Sure." Cat picked the middle restaurant. At least they had decent salads.

It had been so easy interviewing Simon, seeing the mines and the chunks of rock with bits of translucent opal showing through. *That* had been exciting. Even being chased through the rain had been scary but strangely exhilarating. Shopping for baby items and then catching lunch at a franchise was awkward; the easiness they'd once shared was gone.

Once again, her life had been irrevocably changed because she'd let down her guard. Although she loved

Opal with a ferociousness she'd never expected, regret still lingered and fear of the future only grew. She had a dark past that never left her alone, making the thought of raising a baby more than a little daunting.

When they were settled into a booth with Opal next to her, still sleeping in her car seat, Cat quickly scanned the menu and set it down.

"You know what you want?" Simon slowly perused his.

She wanted to be back in New York with its vast selection of places to eat. She wanted to hop a plane to exotic places with her camera and then write about them. She wanted the only responsibility in her life to be handing in a piece on time.

Cat sighed. Those days were gone. "A salad."

Simon looked at her closely. "You look good, Cat. I hope you don't think you need to lose weight or anything."

He had no idea. Her jeans still didn't fit. "It's what I want."

He cocked one eyebrow at her. "Very well."

"Speaking of eating, are you coming for Thanksgiving or not? I'd like to let my mother know."

He set down his menu, glanced at Opal, before zeroing back in on her. "What time?"

"Noon, if you'd like to watch the football game. We usually eat between two and three, during halftime."

"Very well. I'll be there for the game." He looked like he'd bit into a sour lemon.

She smiled because the waitress had arrived to take their orders. She had to give Simon credit for agreeing to face her entire family. Hopefully, it'd go well. For all of them.

Chapter Three

Thanksgiving Day, after driving ten miles north of town, Simon stared at the Zelinsky home. It was well kept and big. Cat had grown up in a nice place on an inland lake, with a large yard and plenty of trees to climb. She'd had everything a kid could ask for.

He hadn't talked to Cat for nearly two days. She hadn't stopped by the shop, but then the past couple of days had been cold and rainy. Not good days to take a little baby out.

He'd called last night to see if there was anything he should bring today, but Cat had told him not a thing. After hanging up, he'd prayed for direction, but Simon still felt adrift. With his troubled family background, how would he be able to relate to the Zelinsky clan? Even he and Cat barely knew each other. What mattered most was Opal's welfare and that was why he was here. He wanted to see the rest of the family his daughter had been born into. The people who would have a role in raising her.

Simon made his way along the slate stonework walkway up to the front porch. Taking a deep breath, he rang the doorbell and waited.

He heard voices and laughter and then the door was

opened by an older woman with classic features and blondish hair, which was pulled back tight. "You must be Simon."

"I am. Thank you for inviting me." He offered her his hand and smiled at the warmth shining from the woman's eyes.

She accepted the handshake. "I'm Helen, Cat's mom, and she's right, that's one great accent you have. Come in, please." She stepped back to give him room to enter. She was about the same middling height as Cat.

He should have told her that she looked more like a sister, but he couldn't get past the fact that Cat liked his accent. Having spent his late teens and most of his adult life living in London, he'd picked up a bit of how they spoke.

What else did Cat find agreeable?

"We've got the game on in the family room. Are you a fan of football?"

"I enjoy watching it, yes." Simon grew up watching the Giants, having been born and raised in New York City.

He followed Cat's mom from the large entrance area into a warm kitchen filled with tempting food aromas and family members huddled around a spread of snacks. The itchy feeling of being the odd man out hit quick and sure. Add that he was Opal's father, and it made him the proverbial white elephant in the room.

Where was Cat?

"Cat's feeding Opal. She'll be down in a moment," her mother answered as if reading his thoughts. "Simon, this is my husband, Andy."

Simon stood straighter, but Cat's father still towered over him. He extended his hand. "Good to meet you, sir."

Cat's father looked through him and Simon was certain the man found him lacking in every way possible as he accepted his hand. "Thank you for coming."

"Your invitation was very kind." Simon saw where Zach got his bearing. He glanced around the room again, wishing Cat would hurry.

Her mother was now busy in the kitchen with Zach's wife and a tall blond man he'd met at church—also one of Cat's brothers.

"We look forward to knowing you better," Andy said.

Simon merely nodded. Too many layers in that statement to uncover each one now. He felt a strong urge to apologize, but the words evaded him. There wasn't much that could be said to expunge what had happened between him and Cat.

Fortunately, Cat's sister Monica scuffled toward him before he made a fool of himself trying to explain the unexplainable to Cat's father.

"Hey, have you considered my website offer?" She too was quite tall. Cat came from a family of giants. "I can do an online catalog that'll knock your socks off."

"I'm closing up shop."

Monica's mouth dropped. "You are? Why? I thought you were doing well."

"Yes, well—"

Cat's father placed his hand on Simon's shoulder. "Grab a plate and come watch the game. We'll talk later."

Simon didn't mistake the hard look in Andy's eyes. Cat's father reduced him to an awkward teen in a matter of moments. He'd known from the start that coming here wasn't going to be easy, but he hadn't expected the tension to be quite this strong.

"Hello, Simon." Cat breezed into the room, grabbed a carrot from one of the trays and popped it into her mouth.

"Where's Opal?"

She pointed to the ceiling, still crunching. "Sleeping."

"What if she wakes up? How will you know?"

"Baby monitor." Cat pulled out what looked like a white walkie-talkie from the pocket of her long top.

She wore gray leggings with woolen socks. Her hair was up, but some of it fell around her face. He loved her hair like that. He wished they were alone. So many things remained unsettled between them. Unsettled in him.

"Have you met everyone?"

"Just your parents, when I arrived."

"Grab a pop. That's my brother Cam in the kitchen with my mom. They pretty much run the show with food prep and the rest of us clean up."

Cam turned and gave him a nod. His hands were deep in a bowl of something.

Simon remembered that he'd seen Cam at the diner in town, as well as in church. Simon picked up a can of soda from an ice-filled tub and followed Cat down a few steps, where everyone was gathered to watch the game. A couple soft couches and chairs were filled, along with a rocking chair near the fireplace. A couple of Cat's brothers lounged against large pillows on the floor, leaving only one two-seater couch open.

"Everyone, this is Simon Roberts."

He nodded as Cat introduced everyone in the room. He'd likely not remember their names, but there was a strong family resemblance. Cat was one of ten kids, with four older brothers and three younger, as well as two younger sisters.

Simon sat next to her on the two-seater, with nothing to say.

Fortunately, he didn't need to say anything, as Cat kept talking. "My brother Matthew is still on the lakes. He's an officer on a Great Lakes freighter, but his wife and her two-year-old will join us for dessert later. Greg there is Rose's son. She married Cam around this time last year."

The teenager gave him a nod. His mother, a warm smile.

Simon had seen them both at the diner, as well. "You've a large family."

"I do." Cat leaned back.

Simon also sat back but didn't relax. The warmth of the fire and conversation surrounded him as he was peppered with well-intentioned questions that he answered the best he could. These people were nice and well-adjusted, a far cry from the world he grew up in. It should have felt comfortable and welcoming—he could tell that was the atmosphere the whole family was trying to create. But instead, it just made him feel out of place.

The desire to bolt overwhelmed him, but the future of one tiny baby kept him seated. Opal slept without a peep from the baby monitor and Cat looked tired. He noticed her eyelids drooping as soon as the football game started.

The desire to make things better for her twisted deep inside, but there wasn't much he could do. With his arm draped along the back of the loveseat, he whispered, "You can lean into me."

"No, no. I'm fine." Cat's eyes met his.

Could she really lean on him, through all of this? He'd given her no reason to, announcing he was closing up shop and skipping town. Sure, he'd offered financial support but how could he give Cat something to truly lean on?

Looking around, he was tempted to foist his responsibility for Opal on these people. Cat had everything she'd need right here.

He'd never had a normal family life. What made him think he'd do any better for Opal than these people? He couldn't, so was there any point in trying?

But what of his daughter? Uncles couldn't take the place of a father and he was her father.

Cat tried to clear the fog from her brain. She rested against someone warm. Inhaling the subtle, spicy scent, she opened her eyes and blinked.

"You weren't out long." Simon's voice was soft and deep and it rumbled through her. That voice of his was her undoing with its buttery half accent and slight lilt of words.

"Sorry." She sat up fast and rubbed her cheek, still warm from where she'd leaned into his shoulder. The shirt he wore was soft flannel, yet the man managed to look fashionable even in that.

She heard her sister's voice through the monitor. If Opal wasn't awake, she would be soon. "I should check on the baby."

He nodded.

She escaped, but not before she connected with her father's concerned gaze. Remembering their argument the last time she was home, she could easily imagine his thoughts. He was thinking she should settle down with Simon because of Opal, but Cat wasn't making any sudden moves. Not when she knew next to nothing about Simon, and he knew so little about her. Even if she wanted a relationship, would Simon be on board for that? He'd said he'd come back, but would he stick around?

She hurried for the stairs.

"Cat, why didn't you tell me it was Simon!" Monica hissed as she came down the steps with Opal in her arms. "I have to admit he's pretty hot for an older guy."

Cat knew her sister was teasing by the way she smirked. It didn't matter that Simon was older than Cat by more than a few years— Wait, she didn't even know his age.

She reached for the baby. "Does she need to be changed?"

"I did it. Don't try to change the subject. I think Mom's a little surprised by his age too, and I think Dad's going to give your man a talking-to."

Cat felt her stomach drop yet again. *Please, not today.* "He's not *my man*."

"Give it time." Monica grinned and carried Opal the rest of the way down the stairs with no moves toward giving her up.

Cat didn't have time where Simon was concerned. He'd severed his lease on his jewelry store effective the first of the year. Would Opal change his mind? Could Cat? Did she even want to? The idea of his sticking around just because he felt obligated was horrible. She didn't want him to feel like he was *stuck* with them—trapped into being part of a family he didn't want and wouldn't have chosen.

When Cat returned to the family room, her mother announced that dinner was ready. Her father had hit the pause button on the TV so they wouldn't miss the rest of the game. He stood and stretched. "Let's gather in the dining room."

"Where's Opal?" Simon asked.

"Monica has her." Cat caught the quick flash of disappointment in his eyes, causing her stomach to twist.

He was forming an attachment to Opal. But was that good or bad? Even though she didn't want him feeling trapped, she also didn't want Simon going back to his old globe-trotting routine. Was there any kind of middle ground? A way he could be part of their lives on a regular basis, without giving up the life that he'd chosen for himself?

Standing in the dining room, Cat watched as her family gathered around the huge table set with Grandma Zelinsky's fine china and crystal goblets. Covered dishes were strategically placed down the middle, but the luscious aroma of turkey gravy and sage stuffing escaped, making her mouth water. It had been a long time since she'd been home for Thanksgiving. She waited for everyone to slip into their usual seats and a lump caught in her throat. This was home, loud and loving and terribly bittersweet.

"Here, you two sit at this end so we can tuck Opal in her bouncer out of the way of traffic." As usual, her mom had everything under control, even seating.

Monica handed Cat the baby.

Simon reached to take the elevated bouncy seat from her mom and positioned it between their chairs. He looked it over while she buckled Opal in. "She won't tip?"

"It's solid." Cat looked away so Simon wouldn't catch her irritation with him questioning her choice. She'd read countless reviews on the item before purchasing it, making sure it was sound and safe for Opal.

"Let's say grace." Her father, at the other end, reached out to hold the hands of her mom on one side and Cam on the other.

Cat clenched her teeth as she reached for Simon's hand.

His thumb brushed over hers, distracting her from the rote prayer she knew by heart. She stared at their clasped hands, remembering the gentle way he'd touched her on their one night together. The way he'd held her. She'd been half-frozen from the cold rain, but his touch had been so warm.

"Amen." Simon lifted his head.

Had he thought about her at all?

Cat pulled her hand away, grateful for the increased noise of chatter and the clatter of serving dishes being passed. She glanced at Simon and nearly laughed at the shocked look upon his face. "Crazy, I know, but this is home."

"Worse than chow time at some mining camps I've been in." He accepted the tray of turkey and offered to fill her plate before his. "White or dark?"

"A little of both, please." Her mother had always made two turkeys so there would be plenty of leftovers. She watched as Simon served her before choosing an ample portion for himself.

"What about Opal, when will she eat solid food?"

Cat's head spun. Thinking back to when her youngest sister Erin and brother Luke were babies, she couldn't remember when they started eating solids. "Honestly, I'm not sure."

Simon stared at her as if she should know these things by heart. "I bought a book."

"A book?"

"About the steps of childhood development over the first year. I purchased it at the local bookstore a couple of stores down from me."

Cat stared at him. Why would he do that? Was he thinking about giving more than financial support?

"What?" His dark eyes looked warm and sweet.

Now wasn't the time to discuss anything in depth, but she had to know. "Why'd you buy that?"

He shrugged. "Honestly, I'm not sure."

Cat looked away and connected with her father's piercing gaze.

Dad's going to give your man a talking-to.

She didn't want her father or Zach making demands on Simon that they had no right to make. She and Simon were too old for her father to pull out the proverbial shotgun, yet that was exactly what he looked like he might do.

* * *

After dinner and cleanup, Cat's family gathered in the family room once again for the remainder of the football game. Simon held Opal in the rocking chair near the fireplace, glad for some distance from Cat. The woman's nearness made his head spin. Not at all a good thing, especially when it made him question everything he'd decided about his future.

He'd put plans in place that were hard to change. Namely, a gem hunt in January for a high-end investor. He couldn't exactly back out and keep his reputation solid. He needed this for future income. Bottom line, he didn't *want* to back out. He loved gem hunting. It was his life—always had been.

He gazed at his daughter's pretty little face as he cradled her in his arms. Holding her might not have been the best idea. He'd used rocking her as a shield against Cat and her family and all that small talk. He wasn't part of the jokes they shared as they loaded the fridge with leftovers and the dishwasher with dirty dishes. He didn't want to be part of them, but using Opal as an excuse for distance had backfired. He'd climbed from one hot pan into another because this baby pulled hard on the heartstrings. This precious little bundle was sinking her sweet little brown-eyed hooks into him fast.

Opal blew bubbles and cooed and kicked her legs. He reached for her hand, amazed at the baby's grip. "You're a strong one."

She gurgled back.

He spotted Cat in the kitchen, talking with one of her sisters-in-law who held a large boy of her own. The child fought to keep his eyes open. Cat's sisters were busy placing pies on the counter and making coffee.

The Lions were down by seventeen, so the game had

lost some of its appeal. Simon glanced around the room.
Cat's younger brothers were sprawled on the floor, sleeping. Even Andy Zelinsky, sitting in a recliner, had closed
his eyes. Zach did too, with his wife, Ginger, cuddled
into him.

What was he even doing here?

Anger he hadn't felt in years roared to life. This was
what a family was supposed to be, was supposed to
have—a warm holiday meal, served with comfortable
trust. No drama, no sirens and no TV dinners. The absence of all of this from his own childhood left him with
a bitter taste in his mouth that no amount of pie they
served could dislodge.

Part of him wanted to make a scene, to vent some of
his anger. But that wouldn't be fair to the people here,
who'd been nothing but welcoming. And it wouldn't be
fair to Opal, who deserved exactly this type of wonderful family occasion. Days like this were things he didn't
want Opal to miss.

Would she grow up missing him?

His gut twisted. If he wasn't careful, he'd miss her.

Simon stopped rocking. Buying that book had only
confirmed that he didn't have what it took to take care
of a baby. One day, he might be of more value than financial child support, but that wasn't now. Cat had a fine
support system in her family right here. She wouldn't be
raising Opal alone.

He carefully stood and crossed the expanse of floor
toward Cat.

"Want me to take her?" Cat asked.

"Please. It's late. I'd better get going." He wanted out.

"But you haven't had dessert." Cat's sister-in-law balanced her boy on her hip.

"Some other time." Simon couldn't get out of there fast enough.

Cat's mom stepped forward and took Opal. "Thank you for coming, Simon. Cat will walk you out."

Cat looked hesitant but nodded. "Yeah, sure."

"Thank you for dinner." He should have said his good-byes to the rest of the family, to Cat's father, but they were sleeping.

At the door, Simon silently donned his coat while Cat slipped into hers and then pulled on a pair of boots. She followed him outside.

The air was crisp with an icy bite to it, but Simon breathed deeply, letting his thoughts settle down. The sun had long since set, leaving behind only remnants of light showing from beneath the dark clouds clustered on the horizon.

"I'll walk you to your car," Cat offered.

"It's cold. You needn't."

"It's okay. I wanted to ask you something, anyway." She looked a little nervous.

That made him want to bolt even faster, but he kept his pace even next to Cat's. "Something on your mind?"

Cat pulled the collar of her coat closer. "Yes. You don't have to give me an answer right away, just think about it."

"What's that?" They were near his car now.

"What if you kept your shop open?"

"I'm committed in January to an investor to buy rubies and tourmaline in Mozambique. It could very well turn into something long-term."

Cat took a deep breath and let it out. "What if I managed your shop for you while you were away?"

He looked at her. "Why would you want to?"

"I gave my notice at the magazine before coming home and I need a job. One that's local."

He narrowed his gaze. "Do you know anything about retail?"

Cat lifted her chin. "How hard can it be?"

He chuckled. Hard enough for him to quit the business after only six months. Though maybe it wasn't that the work was too difficult—it just wasn't something for which he was well suited. He wasn't fond of dealing with customers. He liked finding the goods and making something out of them, but the retail side of things was simply too routine for him. Boring.

"Just think about it." She shivered.

It wasn't a bad idea. "Something to think about."

"Yes, I know."

He ran his hand through his hair. It'd be a way to support Opal as well, keeping tabs on her while she grew up. If Cat succeeded, he would too. He could take payment in gems to use in his own designs while gathering specified items for investors, billing them for travel expenses. His shop lease would have to be reinstated through May. This might work.

She laid her hand on his arm.

Through the heavy wool of his coat, he felt her warmth. Her idea had merit. "What are you doing tomorrow?"

"Not a thing."

"Come by the store before closing and I'll show you what managing a shop would entail."

She searched his eyes, looking worried. "Can I bring the baby?"

It might be better to have the baby along, keeping his mind focused on the reason for all of this. They still needed to discuss support payments, as well. "Yes, that'd be fine."

She grabbed his hand and gave it a squeeze. "Thank you."

He squeezed back. "Good night, Cat."

As he watched her return to the house, a Bible passage he'd read from the gospel of Luke suddenly came to mind.

Whosoever shall seek to save his life shall lose it; and whosoever shall lose his life shall preserve it.

He'd had trouble understanding that verse. Unsure why he thought of it now, Simon searched for meaning and came up empty. Unless…he'd moved to Maple Springs in an attempt to save his life from danger. Perhaps this verse coming to mind confirmed his decision to go back out there.

He was a certified gemologist with a pretty good reputation for finding and purchasing gems. To be the father that his daughter needed, he'd need to provide for her. If he could provide a job for Cat and keep his income stream stable, then all the better.

The tricky thing was his connection to Maple Springs would remain and that might tempt him to linger more than he cared to admit. He'd set up house once before with his siblings and the results had been disastrous for all of them. He didn't want to ruin Opal too. Or Cat.

Chapter Four

Gray clouds darkened the day, making five o'clock seem more like midnight than twilight. Cat stood outside of Simon's jewelry store and shivered. The business card he'd given her showed the store hours as 12:00 p.m. to 6:00 p.m., Tuesday through Saturday.

Cat pulled the collar of her coat closer as a blast of cold air zipped down her neck. She should have worn a scarf. She fiddled with the fleece baby blanket, making sure it still covered Opal in her car seat.

Simon's storefront was small, but he had a large window that showcased his wares. Necklaces, bracelets and rings were meticulously displayed on velvety forms. She looked closer at the gemstones glittering in the overhead lighting. Several of the engagement ring settings were unique with soft folds of silver or gold cradling gorgeous diamonds, emeralds or rubies.

"Like what you see?" Simon's soft accent warmed her as he peeked out from the shop door.

Cat straightened. "I do."

"Good." He grinned and then spotted the car seat and frowned. "Come inside, where it's warm."

Cat stepped inside and it *was* warm. Really warm. "Do you have the heat on high in here?"

He chuckled. "This place doesn't spread the heat well. The back shop is pretty chilly. Let me take your coat."

Cat handed it over and then stooped to take off the blanket covering Opal, who gurgled and smiled. Cat played a quick game of peekaboo, earning another baby smile.

Simon peered down into the car seat. "Hello, Princess."

The baby kicked her feet in response. Evidently, Opal liked Simon's voice too.

"She's very happy today." Cat looked around.

The shop wasn't so much wide as deep. A long display case ran alongside the wall opposite a small counter with a cash register. Behind that was an open area with a large jeweler's workbench and tools and equipment that Cat assumed were used to cut and polish stones, and craft the metal for the settings.

Simon hung her coat on the rack next to his woolen tweed. "Why don't you bring Opal over here? So she's off the floor and away from the draft of the door if someone comes in."

Cat hoisted the car seat and set Opal on a sturdy bench behind the cash register. "I hope I didn't come too early. I know you close at six."

"Perfect timing. Go ahead and look around—you need to get a feel for all that's on display, anyway."

Simon used all sorts of precious and semiprecious gemstones with gold or silver or both. He even displayed jewelry highlighting Northern Michigan finds of Petoskey stone and Leland bluestone.

Cat pointed. "Did you make those?"

"Every piece in here."

"Where'd you get the local stones?" She could easily

imagine Simon scouring the shoreline. Had someone shown him how to spot them?

"Rather curious, aren't they? I'd never heard of them before moving here, but after tourists asked for them, I figured I'd give them a try. I found a guy in Petoskey who has a large supply of raw stones. The Leland blue were some that I found on the beaches there this past summer. A local showed me what to look for and said they were nothing more than leftover smelting slag."

Cat knew that. She'd grown up here. Perusing his display case, she had to give him credit. "Ginger was right, your designs are amazing."

"Thank you."

"How did you maintain your craft at this level when you were hunting for gems?" She reverted to a journalism tone, but she really wanted to know. She wanted to know a lot more about this man.

"I worked in London and New York making jewelry for part of the year so I didn't get rusty. My employer had jewelry stores in each city."

Cat looked over rubies, diamonds, star sapphires and topaz, but one stone was missing. "No opals. Did you sell them?"

"I have them still."

"But no jewelry from them?"

Simon shrugged. "Not yet. Come, I'll show you the ones I kept from the stash I purchased that night."

Cat glanced at the baby. She cooed and kicked, fixated on the large ball of a light fixture overhead. Cat followed Simon into the back of the shop, which was much larger than the front. Cooler too. This was where he made the magic happen, shaping a lump of gemstone into something beautiful. Something unique.

He opened the door of a large safe and pulled out a

tray of plastic bags containing what looked like hunks of rock from a distance. These were the same opals she remembered with flashes of translucent color showing through in spots.

Cat reached out to touch one that Simon laid in front of her. "They are beautiful."

"That one was the largest raw opal of the lot, remember? The best of the best." He touched the rock too, and his finger swiped hers.

Remember?

As if she'd ever forget. She'd accompanied Simon to purchase these. There had been government officials following their every move it seemed, although none of them were around when those three men had chased them for miles. The next morning, Simon had been so quiet when he'd put her on that small plane back to Nairobi. Telling her only that he wanted her out of Ethiopia.

Away from him.

He'd mentioned that they'd both had their reasons for not contacting each other. Cat pulled her hand back. "Why didn't you call me? I didn't know if you were even alive."

Simon looked her in the eyes, but his expression was closed. "I thought about it, but at the time we were worlds apart. I read the article you'd sent to my employer for review, so I knew you'd made it home."

He gave nothing away, not even a hint of what he'd felt about her back then. If anything. What had she expected? It wasn't as if they'd made any sort of commitment…but there had been a connection. She'd felt it as clearly as if it had been a tangible cord that had coiled around them.

Not now, though. He was closed up tight and distant.

"Did you like it? The article."

The corner of Simon's mouth curved into a hint of a

smile, but he didn't answer. The bell of the front door jingled, announcing a customer. "I'll be right back."

She watched him with an older woman looking for a Christmas gift for her daughter. Simon asked the usual questions to get a sense of what the woman might like to see before pulling a tray of sparkly necklaces out from the display case.

An awkward silence filled the space while Simon waited for the woman to choose. Finally, he asked, "Did you want to see something else, perhaps?"

The woman looked at Simon, helplessly uncertain. "Well…"

Cat had a hunch the woman couldn't afford the options Simon had shown her yet was too embarrassed to say so. She finally stepped in. "We have some lovely local stones displayed here if you'd like to have a look."

"Why yes, thank you." The woman's eyes widened and she followed Cat.

Cat discreetly flipped the gilded price tags on several items so the woman didn't have to ask. The woman finally chose a sterling silver and Petoskey stone bracelet.

"I'll have this boxed for you." Cat handed it over to Simon. She took the opportunity to murmur quietly, "Sorry, but I—"

He waved her whispered apology aside as the woman met them at the cash register. It was clear to her already that Simon was hardly a natural at retail sales. She was surprised that his gem-hunting days making deals hadn't helped him gain the skill to read customers. Maybe he simply was too used to playing the waiting game, letting the other person make their move first.

"She's my only child and I still like to spoil her when I get the chance." The woman smiled as she offered her credit card and accepted the bagged jewelry.

Cat glanced at Simon standing nearby. He gazed at Opal and even smiled at the bubble the baby blew.

Once the woman left, Cat faced him. "She couldn't afford those designs you showed her."

Simon's eyebrow lifted. "I'm no mind reader, but I would have figured that out eventually."

Cat didn't think so, or if he had, it would have been too late—after the woman had decided the store was out of her price range and left. "How are sales?"

He shrugged. "Not bad for a first year."

"Do you advertise?"

"No. I haven't yet. Your sister wants to design a store website."

"She's good, plus I can write a pretty mean ad." Cat would have no trouble describing his jewelry in a way that would interest customers. With her sister's help in setting up an online presence, she could take this shop to the next level. If Simon agreed.

"I'm sure you can." Simon checked his watch.

Cat tried to keep the conversation going. "Why close at all?"

"Why?" Simon's brow lifted again. He ran his finger down Opal's cheek and shrugged. "I miss my old life. I'm not good with customers and certainly not used to a small community."

That didn't seem like a good reason, so she dug deeper. "What made you choose jewelry as a career?"

His gaze turned cool. "A series of circumstances, really. My mom kicked me out the summer I turned seventeen. I couldn't find full-time work and ended up living in a park."

Cat absorbed the information, forcing herself not to react. "Why'd she kick you out?"

"She said I was old enough to take care of myself."

Cat was floored. "What about school? Couldn't they help?"

"Like I said, it was summer."

"What did you do? How did you eat?"

Simon's expression hardened. "Dumpsters, day-old stuff from a bakery. Finally, a man hired me to clean up his workshop in exchange for lodging if I agreed to finish high school. He happened to be a master bench jeweler for the company I eventually worked for. I apprenticed with him in London and eventually pursued an education in gemology."

"I see." She remembered when she was first interviewing him back in Ethiopia, asking him about his personal story to no avail. He'd changed the subject, preferring to remain on the topic of opals. Now she understood why.

Everyone has a past. Some worse than others. Having been through darkness herself, she'd learned to cope. Regardless of the challenges she faced in coming home, she needed a job and he needed a way to provide for Opal. This seemed to take care of both. Spending time together didn't mean they'd have to dig into their dark pasts. Some things might be better left buried.

He went to the door and locked it. "Closing time."

"Well, what do you think of my idea?"

"It has some merit."

"Should we discuss it over dinner? There's a good Chinese restaurant with takeout in the plaza near the high school. I can pick it up and meet you at your house."

"You're not giving up."

Cat smiled. "Nope."

"Call in the order, and I'll pick it up and meet you at my place."

"Perfect." Cat reached for her phone while Simon took care of closing up the shop.

* * *

Simon didn't share his childhood stories lightly. He didn't know why telling Cat left him feeling so uneasy. She'd grown up with everything he didn't have—a loving family and a beautiful place to live, while he'd had so little by comparison. He had regrets that chased him still. Regrets he feared.

"I'll tell you what." Simon reached into the cash register, drew out a key and handed it to her. "This is a spare key to my house. Why don't you take Opal and get settled in?"

Cat stared at the key.

He remembered her looking exactly that way standing in the middle of the hut they had holed up in, shivering.

"Take the key, Cat."

"Right." She shook off whatever had stalled her and scooped it out of his palm. "See you in a bit."

He picked up her coat and held it open for her. She hesitated a moment, searching his eyes. What she looked for, he couldn't guess. Scared of the answer, he didn't ask. "I won't be long," he told her.

"Okay." She turned and slipped her arms into the garment.

He folded down the upturned collar and smoothed his hands over her shoulders. He breathed in the soft scent of Cat's hair and managed to keep from leaning in closer. Barely. He would, though. He had to. They had too much to work out between them. He watched her and Opal leave before closing the door.

He'd left all those raw opals out and needed to return them to the safe, where they would stay until he figured out what to do with them. He picked up the largest of the stones, enjoying the fire that flashed from deep within.

It truly was the best he'd seen in Welo opals, maybe any opal anywhere.

He turned the stone in his hand. Every time he'd considered polishing this one or any of the opals he'd purchased with Cat alongside him, he'd change his mind. Especially this large one. The best one.

Perhaps he'd make something for Cat out of these. A pendant maybe, set on a chunky silver chain. No, platinum. An image of a ring entered his thoughts, making his gut pitch.

Proposing marriage was out of the question. He didn't know how to be a father, much less a husband. He was too used to being alone. Too used to running from anyone who wanted more from him than he could give. He wouldn't make it as a family man. He'd tried it, long after he'd left New York when his siblings faced foster care.

Battling with that failure was a different type of fear. Different even than memories of his childhood. Not having two dependable parents in his life threw fuel on his resolve to be involved in Opal's life somehow. No, he didn't know how to be a father, and no, he wasn't meant to be a family man—but he wasn't going to abandon his daughter. He wouldn't let himself be that man. He might be incredibly incompetent as a father, but he would still find a way to be part of her life. As long as he didn't mess her up.

Maybe having Cat manage the retail side of the shop was a way to do that. He'd have his distance, and yet keeping an inventory meant coming back to Maple Springs.

Cat entered Simon's house carting Opal in her car seat and with the diaper bag slung over her shoulder. Setting both on the floor, she closed the door, hit the light switch and hung up her coat in the small entry closet. The place was still neat as a pin. And bare.

She settled Opal's car seat in the middle of the living room floor and then headed for the kitchen. She deposited a couple of filled baby bottles from her diaper bag into the fridge. She hoped to get Opal taking a bottle before she started work. She'd asked her mother when Opal might begin eating solid food and her answer had been cereal in a few weeks, when Opal was nearing four months old.

She heard Opal fussing in the living room. "Hang on, baby."

Opal cried louder.

Cat's body reacted even though she'd fed Opal before she left her parents' place. Gathering up the baby, Cat shed the blanket and Opal quieted. "I'm sorry. Were you too hot?"

The baby gurgled and squalled a little.

Cat ran her finger down the side of her daughter's cold cheek. It wasn't that warm in Simon's house. Cat spread the fleece blanket on the thick area rug in the middle of the floor and then settled Opal on her belly. "Let's get a fire started."

Opal cooed and kicked her legs.

Cat chuckled and rubbed the baby's back. "You look like a little frog, not a princess."

More cooing.

Cat checked that the damper of the fireplace was open, and then she stacked some kindling from the wood box next to the hearth. She retrieved matches from the mantel and lit the pile. The flames caught quickly, licking the dry wood, making it snap and crackle. She watched the fire spread and then tossed on a couple of small logs. She'd have to buy him a protective fireplace screen. But then, he wasn't planning to stay.

Rolling her shoulders, Cat looked around. Out of the windows, she saw the distant glow of the sunset peeking out from under dark clouds. The house was quiet save for the sounds of burning wood. Home had been full of noise when she left. Between her little brother Luke's stereo blaring and her youngest sister, Erin, moving back in, Cat was glad for a chance to escape. For an evening, anyway. Even though it meant an awkward evening spent with Simon.

Cat's stomach flipped when she heard the door open.

The man of her thoughts entered holding a large paper bag. He stood terribly still and stared.

She stared back. Was something wrong? "I hope you don't mind that I started a fire."

He closed the door. "No, I'm glad you did. It'll take the chill off. Thank you."

"You're welcome." She reached for the bag so he could slip out of his coat. "I'll take this to the kitchen."

"Thank you." Simon didn't look at her, though. He went straight for Opal and knelt down next to her. "Hello."

Cat watched as Opal twisted her head toward his voice. That quick movement made her teeter and roll, right onto her side.

"Whoa, not so quick there, Princess." Simon righted her back onto her belly. His nickname for Opal was rather sweet.

Cat continued into the kitchen, heart racing. She opened the paper bag and inhaled the delicious smell of the takeout, which made her stomach rumble. Eat first, and then talk. "Do you want me to plate this up now while it's still hot?"

"I'll help you. Can she stay on the floor like this?"

"Yes. Or we can put her in the car seat while we eat."

He threw a couple more logs on the fire before returning to Opal on the floor. "You want to come pick her up?"

Cat noticed that he looked completely out of his element. "Didn't you ever pick up your brother or sister?"

He shook his head. "Not much when they were little babies and, well, it's been a long time."

He hadn't been afraid running from those would-be thieves, but lifting a little one off the floor seemed too much for him. "I'll show you how to lift her."

His eyes widened, but he didn't refuse.

Cat left the take-out containers on the kitchen table. Walking past Simon, she knelt on the floor and gently scooped Opal up, supporting her neck while she turned the baby in her arms. "See?"

Simon knelt next to her. "Okay, lay her back down."

Cat did so, ready to get up when Simon touched her arm, sending a shiver straight to her shoulder.

"Stay a minute. Make sure I do this right." He repeated the same motion and Opal smiled up at him.

"She likes that."

He laid her back down and did it again with a faster, swinging motion.

Opal cooed.

"She's going to need her father, you know." Cat's thoughts slipped into spoken words.

Simon looked at her with a stark expression. "I'm not sure I can be what she needs."

Cat knew that feeling all too well. "I'll set the table."

Simon stood too and settled the baby back in her car seat. "Where do you want her?"

"Next to my chair is fine." Cat dug in the diaper bag for a mobile that clipped onto the car seat, to keep the baby entertained.

Opal's gaze latched on to the stuffed zebra and giraffe overhead. She reached for a toy and missed it, her little arm arching wildly off the mark.

Simon guided her tiny hand to the toy and gently shook it, making the inner rattle click. That earned a bubble-blowing coo. He chuckled and shook the rattle again.

Cat turned away, her throat tight. Opal didn't ask to be born, but she deserved both parents in her life. Cat might have been wrong in keeping Opal a secret from Simon, but now that he knew, he was wrong to think he had so little to offer her.

She searched the cupboards for glasses until she gained control of her emotions. "What do you want to drink?"

"Water's fine." Simon continued to play with Opal.

Opal started to fuss and Cat sighed, running the tap water till it went ice-cold. Surely the baby wasn't hungry so soon. Over the snap and crackle of the fire blazing in the hearth, she heard Simon singing. Softly. The tune and words were unfamiliar.

"While the moon her watch is keeping, All through the night. While the weary world is sleeping, All through the night.

"O'er thy spirit gently stealing, visions of delight revealing breathes a pure and holy feeling, All through the night."

She set two glasses of water on the table and listened. He repeated the tune, humming instead of singing as his gaze slammed into hers. Cat held her breath. How on earth did Simon know a lullaby?

Cat glanced at Opal. Like her, the baby was mesmerized by his deep, smooth voice. Then Opal kicked and waved her arms. "She wants you to keep singing."

Simon lifted Opal still in the car seat and set her on the table. "That's enough for now, I think."

Cat wouldn't mind hearing more. "What was that? I've never heard it before."

"A lullaby my mom used to sing. I guess I remembered

the words." Simon had said that his mother had passed away a few years ago.

"I'm sorry she's gone." Such inadequate words. "For you, I mean."

He gave her an odd look. "I grew up in an unpleasant situation. My mother was an addict who couldn't stay clean for very long."

Cat's stomach clenched at the contempt in his voice. "Oh."

Simon shrugged. "Let's eat, shall we?"

Cat sat down, her appetite gone. His mother's addiction explained a lot about why he seemed so closed off. He'd been uncomfortable at her parents' house for Thanksgiving. He must have a mountain of bad childhood memories, culminating in having been kicked out at seventeen. Hadn't Ginger thought him lonely?

Simon reached out, his hand palm up on the table. "Let's pray first."

Cat resisted the urge to decline. Praying like they were a real family seemed too intimate, and odd that he'd choose to hold hands when he was so guarded. Finally, she slipped her hand over his, relieved when he held on loosely.

Simon bowed his head. "Thank you, Lord, for this food and please give us wisdom in this situation. Amen."

Short and sweet. Cat pulled her hand away. "We've definitely created a situation."

"Indeed." Simon opened the take-out containers and offered her a choice between moo goo gai pan and peppered beef. "We'll figure it out."

"You keep saying that." Cat took the containers and scooped a little of both onto her plate. "How? Opal might be young enough right now not to miss you when you leave, but what about when she's older?"

He blew out his breath. "Something to consider."

Cat set down her fork. "Opal will need more than simply financial support."

He looked at her hard. "And what about you?"

Cat looked away. "I need a job. Hiring me to manage your store will kill two birds with one stone. It'll give me financial stability and give you a reason to come back here and spend time with your daughter."

"All right, let's give it a trial run. Help me run the shop, starting next week, and we'll see."

Cat nodded. "Can I bring the baby with me?"

Simon looked a little surprised. "If this works, you won't be able to bring her every day, you know, after I'm gone."

"I know." Cat might as well be honest. "I have a hard time leaving her. Even with my mother, who's the only one I trust watching her, it's still hard, and if I can ease into it—"

He held up his hand as if he didn't want to know the details. "Understood."

Opal scrunched her face and squalled, reaching toward the food. She seemed highly indignant that no one was sharing it with her.

"Hush now, Princess, you're not old enough to eat this." Simon touched the toys dangling overhead to capture her attention. It worked. Opal quieted and reached for them again. She missed again too.

"You're good with her." Cat considered the next couple of weeks a trial period with Simon too.

For Opal's sake, she didn't want Simon leaving, never to return. It had nothing to do with her needs or wants or even interest in him sticking around. This wasn't about the two of them anymore. Cat was determined to do what was best for one of them. Opal.

Chapter Five

After dinner, Simon cleaned up while Cat attended to a fussy Opal.

"Hey, look, it's snowing," Cat said.

He stopped what he was doing and looked outside. Through the wide windows, snowflakes fell, glittering with reflections from the outside light left on. The snow was light, not the kind that promised to pile up. That snow would soon come, though, reminding him that winter was closing in—and time was ticking.

His landlord had agreed to sever the lease, but the guy wouldn't return to the area until spring. He wouldn't actively look for replacement tenants until then. The house had been easy to break as rentals were snapped up rather quickly.

He glanced at Cat looking out the windows as she rocked the baby. Their baby. The fleece blanket covered half of them.

"I can throw another log on the fire if you're cold."

Cat's stormy gaze met his. "She wouldn't take the bottle, so…"

It hit him that Cat was feeding Opal and the room seemed to shrink in on him. Same feeling he'd experienced when he entered his house to a fire in the grate and Cat and Opal waiting for him like they belonged here. Like *he* belonged here too, with them. Only, he didn't.

He cleared his throat, and then he settled on the couch and picked up the baby book he had left there. He focused on the pages, wanting to give Cat at least the illusion of privacy, and needing a little distance from the intimate family scene.

"All clear. Sorry, I should have used your other room."

Simon held up the baby book. "Have you read anything like this?"

Cat looked uncomfortable. "No. I'd read the book before it, though—the pregnancy one—while I was expecting."

"Perhaps you should. Perhaps you shouldn't switch to a bottle just yet."

"I have to before I return to work and you leave. You said so yourself, once you're gone and I'm covering the store, I can't have Opal there with me. She'll need to be used to a bottle if she's going to stay home with my mom." Cat looked cross, as if he had no business telling her what to do.

He didn't, and for some reason that got under his skin, as well. "I'd like to be part of the decisions that affect her. That's all I'm saying."

Cat's eyes narrowed. "It's not your body that reacts every time she cries."

He'd overstepped, way overstepped. Simon spread his hands wide. "I apologize. I simply want what's best for her."

Cat stood and shifted Opal to her shoulder. She softly patted the baby's back. "Do you? You're leaving in a month with no indication when you're coming back."

He winced at that truth but rallied. "You never told me

about Opal, so what difference does it make if I'm here or not? At least at this stage."

Cat opened her mouth as if to say something, but didn't. She let out her breath in a whoosh. "Maybe I'd better go."

"Why?"

They stood glaring at each other and he wondered where this sudden anger came from.

Opal burped and it was loud.

It cut the tension and Simon couldn't help but smile.

Cat sort of smiled too and bundled up Opal into the car seat. "You know what? We can do this another time."

"Fine," Simon agreed.

It was no use arguing, not when he wasn't sure what they truly argued over. Was it his leaving or caring what happens to Opal? Perhaps it was a mix of both that bothered Cat.

Cat bundled up the baby before she grabbed her coat and the diaper bag, and then headed back for the car seat.

"I'll take her to the car. Your hands are full."

Cat nodded. "Thank you."

He scooped up his daughter, looking cute in a pink fleece hat with matching booties and mittens, along with the fleece blanket, and followed Cat out the door. It had stopped snowing, so at least he didn't have to worry about her driving in it.

Sliding the car seat into place, he ran his finger down the baby's cheek. Then he glanced at Cat. "Drive carefully."

She rolled her eyes and started the engine.

He backed away and shut the car door, watching her pull away faster than he thought was necessary. Leaving might be stickier than he'd imagined.

* * *

The next day, Simon debated whether to call Cat and apologize. Perhaps he'd said things he had no right to say. And yet he didn't call, because while he was sorry he'd overstepped, he couldn't claim he'd never do it again. He still wanted to be included when it came to Opal. As a Christian man, it was the right thing to do. Another right thing to do was hire Cat to manage his shop and leave it open for now.

First thing this morning, he'd contacted both landlords to let them know he'd see his full year's lease through to the end of May. They'd been relieved that he'd changed his mind about severing the leases early. Simon still planned to leave in January, but he'd be back after finishing his assignment at the very least to figure out the next step for his business.

The door jingled and Zach Zelinsky entered, looking like a storm cloud. He gave Simon a nod. "You busy?"

Simon narrowed his gaze. "Not at the moment."

Zach shifted his stance. "Look, I might have overreacted at church, but Cat's my sister."

"I understand." Simon nearly chuckled at the apology, grudgingly given.

"So what are you going to do about it? Cat and the baby."

Simon bit back the desire to tell Zach that it was none of his business. He appreciated Zach's protective big-brother role. He appreciated that the Zelinskys were a tight family, a good family, but whatever happened between him and Cat was private.

"I'm still trying to figure that out," Simon finally said.

"Cat hasn't had it easy." Zach looked at his feet.

Had Cat been in bad relationships before or was he alluding to having Opal? "She's a strong woman."

Zach looked at him hard. "You have no idea. I'm here for two reasons. First, Ginger wanted me to invite you to our place later tonight, after the tree-lighting ceremony, for a family get-together."

Simon tried to read between those lines and came up empty. Obviously, Cat's family was reaching out to him because of Opal. Perhaps it really was as simple as that. "Tree lighting?"

"It's been a town tradition for as long as I can remember. The first Saturday night after Thanksgiving, Maple Springs ushers in the Christmas season with a community tree lighting."

Simon nodded. "And the second?"

Zach gave him a bit of a sheepish grin. "What do you have in rubies?"

Simon raised his eyebrows. "For Ginger?"

"Yeah. For Christmas. She's been talking about your stuff since you opened. I might be thickheaded, but sooner or later even I can take a hint."

Simon chuckled as he opened the case and withdrew several ruby pendants set in white gold, along with bracelets and earrings. "I can design a different setting if you don't find something you like here."

"I wouldn't begin to know what to ask for." Zach looked over the merchandise, checking prices, and then he stopped. "That one."

Simon pointed at a necklace with a square cut ruby that was set in white gold that wrapped over the front of the stone like an embrace. He'd mused it was a lover's piece when he'd designed it. "The price on this one—"

"Doesn't matter. That's Ginger, all right. I'll take the earrings to match."

It was middling priced, but Simon discounted it when he rang it up. "There you go."

Zach zeroed in on the receipt and shook his head. "Thanks. You didn't have to do that, but I appreciate it. See you later, then?"

Simon wasn't exactly glad to go, but he needed to smooth things over with Cat. They hadn't parted well last night. "Yes. I'll be there."

"Good."

Simon watched Zach leave, but his words about Cat replayed through his mind. According to Zach, she'd had a rough time of it and he had no idea about Cat's strength. Was it simply a matter of speech or was there something else concerning Opal that Cat hadn't told him?

Perhaps tonight he'd find out.

Cat slipped into a coat borrowed from her mom. She was the only one who'd ridden to Zach's with her parents, since his place was a short walk to Center Park and the tree lighting. Her brothers and sisters would meet them in town. It had been years since she'd last attended a Maple Springs Christmas tree lighting and part of her looked forward to it. The other part didn't.

Coming home to stay, she'd known that she'd run into people she'd grown up with. People who knew her past. People who remembered Muriel Jensen's drowning. Nearly every day for the past fifteen years, Cat woke up remembering the face of that three-year-old girl. Every day she practiced the coping lessons she'd learned in counseling, but her guilt didn't always stay packed away.

Tonight she'd draw on those lessons even more. Running into Simon had distracted her from a lot of that anxiety, but tonight those concerns took front and center. People who knew her and her past would be at the tree lighting.

"Ready?" Her mom squeezed her arm before caressing Opal's cheek.

Opal was snuggled into a stretchy wrap against Cat's chest. Her mom's old down coat was roomy enough for Cat to fasten over the bulge the baby made in front. She'd win no prizes for style, but Opal would stay warm.

"What if I see people who know?" Cat couldn't keep the tremor out of her voice.

Her mom gave her a sympathetic smile. "It'll be okay, Cat. A lot of years have passed."

"People don't forget."

"No, but they forgive."

Cat chewed her lip. It had to be done. If only she shared her mother's confidence, but really, what person forgives the unforgivable? She secured a supersoft fleece hat on Opal's head.

The baby gurgled and smiled. She didn't mind the soft ties under her chin or the matching fleece mittens that went with the fleece romper Cat had put on her. According to Cat's mom, Opal was a very good baby. A blessing.

Cat took a deep breath.

"She's so cute," Cat's mom said.

"She is, but I look like the Marshmallow Man." Cat pulled her own hat down over her ears and then looped her camera over her shoulder. If managing Simon's store didn't work out, she'd try freelance writing and photography work for domestic travel magazines or whatever else she could find. This could make a nice piece.

Her mother caressed Cat's cheek. "You look wonderful."

"You're a bad liar, Mom." Cat followed her mother outside.

Her mother froze, looking far too serious. "I don't lie."

"I was only teasing." Cat had never known her mom

to tell a falsehood, other than when she'd comforted Cat
after the drowning, telling her it'd be all right.

It had never been all right. Tonight the sting felt fresh
again, like an old splinter that rose to the surface of her
flesh only to snag on everything she touched.

Once outside, big snowflakes silently fell from a wind-
less sky. The air felt mild and not too cold to be outside.
Perfect for Opal's first tree lighting. Perfect for taking
pictures of a quaint resort town that knew how to cele-
brate the holidays.

Despite the sound of distant laughter, there was also
a slight hush covering the town as if in anticipation for
what was yet to come. This was nothing like the hustle
and bustle of the big tree lighting in New York's Rockefeller Center. Maple Springs treated this night with more
reverence as the official opening of the Christmas season.

"Come on, dawdlers." Her brother Cam walked ahead
of them with his wife, Rose.

"You go on." Her mother waved him away.

Cat savored this short walk with some of her family. She gawked at the white Christmas lights swirled on
every tree that lined Main Street and stopped to snap a
few photos. The storefronts were decorated with more
lights and some had little Christmas trees out front with
candy canes and golden apples. Classic evergreen wreaths
with big red velvet bows hung from nearly every door.

She glanced at Simon's jewelry shop window, bare but
for the glittering of gemstones. The store was dark beyond the window display lights. Was he at home, alone?

Cat should have called and apologized for leaving the
previous night the way she did. She'd been miffed at him
trying to tell her how to parent her child, using some book
he'd purchased as *the* source of sage advice. Her mom

was her go-to for information. Having raised ten kids, her mom knew far more than any developmental book.

"Hello, Catherine Zelinsky." Simon's deep purr of a voice sounded next to her.

She stopped walking and faced him. "Where did you come from?"

He didn't answer. Simon peered into the front of her coat. "Is that Opal in there?"

The baby jerked her head toward his voice.

Simon looked surprised and maybe even a little moved as he rubbed the baby's cheek. "She knows me. Do you have her tied up in a scarf?"

"No, it's a wrap-styled baby carrier. Good for infants. She'll stay warmer this way." A gift from a coworker, and Cat was glad she'd finally used it after figuring out how to tie the thing.

"Good idea." Simon didn't look away from her. "Cat, I'm sorry about last night."

She smiled. "Yeah, me too."

He smiled back.

She looked away, toward his shop. "You need to decorate your storefront. The Winter Shoppers' Walk is a week away, next Saturday night."

"I'm not into that sort of thing."

"I am."

He gave her a half smile. "Very well, your first duty as shop manager."

Cat tamped down the sudden tipsy sensation that soared through her. "So, you're not closing?"

"No. Not yet. I'll see it through to the end of my lease in May. It makes sense, since I can't possibly sell everything in so short a time."

"So, are you still leaving?"

Simon's gaze remained steady. "In January, yes, until

I can finish the job I've already contracted to do. I'll be able to pick up some more inventory at the same time. By keeping the store open, I'll need more gemstones, and going for them myself cuts out the middleman."

Cat didn't like the disappointment that simple statement caused. It wasn't as if she expected him to stay by her side all the time. It wasn't as if there was a relationship between them. They were two people who'd made an error in judgment because of crazy circumstances that resulted in a baby. Now she'd be his employee. That didn't quite feel right either.

"Come on, or we'll miss the lighting of the tree." Cat wasn't sure what she wanted.

He stalled her with a touch to her arm. "I'm going to Zach's after. That's not a problem for you, is it?"

"No, of course not. Just because we disagreed, doesn't mean I'm mad at you. We'll probably disagree a lot."

"I suppose we will." He gave her a teasing grin.

She ignored the sense that maybe he'd look forward to that. Or was it making up after? Cat tamped down the butterflies that line of thought aroused. She tucked her arm in his as they crossed the street. "Come on, let's go."

So far, she hadn't run into anyone she knew and that was fine by her. They joined the rest of her family gathered around the gigantic pine tree. It was tough to recognize people bundled in hats and heavy coats.

Simon didn't fit the typical Maple Springs merchant wearing his tailored dark tweed peacoat. No one wore those around here. He didn't wear a hat either, but a knitted scarf wrapped around his neck. Another fashionable look that screamed not from around here.

He caught her staring, so she looked away as the chamber of commerce president awkwardly tapped the microphone, causing it to squeal.

The crowd groaned. A few people even hollered out jeers.

The president gestured to whomever was handling the sound in a rather condescending manner and Cat couldn't believe this was the guy who had captured Monica's interest. Surely it was a passing thing.

"Good evening, and thank you for joining us for the Maple Springs annual Christmas tree-lighting ceremony…"

Caught up in the festive atmosphere, Cat cheered right along with the rest of the crowd. It earned her a shocked glance from Simon and a grimace from Opal.

The baby puckered up, ready to cry.

"Hush, baby. Shhh." Cat gently bounced her and she quieted. "This is fun, don't you think?"

"It is rather fun." Simon gave her a smile that warmed all the way down to her toes.

The chamber president continued, "My assistant, Monica, will get us started on a couple of songs before we count down to lighting the tree."

"Hey, that's your sister." Simon nodded.

"Yes." She joined in when Monica began to sing "Jingle Bells."

"Your family is into everything here."

"For as long as I can remember." Cat resumed singing.

Her father's side of the family had lived in this town for generations. Zelinskys had always attended the largest church in Maple Springs with deep ties to the community. Her brothers might attend elsewhere, but her parents still went and often volunteered for church functions and fund-raisers that benefited everyone, not only the parish.

Cat looked over the crowd singing their hearts out as they moved on to another carol.

"We wish you a Merry Christmas. We wish you a Merry Christmas…" they sang in unison.

Cat soaked it in. She'd always loved Christmastime. It was the only time of year when she'd sometimes forget the past. From the hustle of holiday shopping to Christmas movies and decorating a tree, Cat greedily immersed herself in the season.

Looking around, she noted that the people here were business owners, teachers and workers—year-round residents who made up the backbone of Maple Springs. The ones who made this town attractive to summer people and tourists. The beauty of Maple Bay had a lot to do with it too, but there was warmth here and something harder to name.

She quickly snapped a couple of photos, hoping to capture the essence of this moment. Maple Springs was a place where people weren't afraid to sing real Christmas carols. All things she'd point out in her article.

This was why she'd come home. She wanted Opal raised in this warmth, and she hoped it would rewrap around her, as well. Her mother said people forgave in time. Could that be possible? Could she ever truly forgive herself?

"You stopped singing." Simon moved closer to her. "Everything okay?"

She searched for something to say and blurted, "This is way different compared to the lighting at Rockefeller Center."

"Smaller tree," Simon teased.

Cat laughed. "Not just that, but there's a warmth here, don't you think? Did you go to this sort of thing in London or New York?"

"If I wasn't scouting out gemstones somewhere, I was

working late to fill custom orders, so no. December was the store's busiest time of year in both locations."

"Right. Lots of people buy jewelry for Christmas." She thought about the lady she'd helped purchase a bracelet. If left to his own devices, Simon might have lost that sale. No wonder he'd wanted to close up shop. He wasn't a retailer.

"…We wish you a Merry Christmas and a Happy New Year." The second carol ended and the crowd cheered.

The chamber president turned on the microphone, generating another squeal. "On the count of three, Monica will flip the switch."

The crowd counted with him. "One…two…three!"

The Center Park pine tree burst into jam-packed colored-light glory.

Cat's throat grew tight. Ever since Opal had been born, she grew emotional over the least little thing. She snapped a few more quick photos. Scooting over for a better angle, she accidentally brushed into someone.

That someone turned around. "Cat, is that you?"

The familiar voice made her stomach drop as if she were on an elevator going down too fast. "Mrs. Jensen!"

The woman whose life Cat had ruined stood before her. It had been years and yet the sorrow in Sue Jensen's eyes hadn't changed. Sorrow Cat had put there.

"Is this your husband? Oh, and you have a baby!"

Her breath hitched at Mrs. Jensen's astonished tone. Cat knew she didn't deserve a healthy baby, or even happiness. "This is Opal."

Simon, still standing close, draped his arm around Cat's shoulders as he reached out to Mrs. Jensen. "How do you do, I'm Simon."

Mrs. Jensen didn't take his hand, choosing to grip each

of their arms instead. "Congratulations to you both and Merry Christmas."

"Merry Christmas." Cat didn't recognize her own voice due to the low rawness of it.

Staring at Sue Jensen's retreating back, Cat stumbled into the past. Too clearly, she remembered the way the woman had wailed over the body of her dead daughter. Cat had collapsed on the dock after repeated attempts at CPR and mouth-to-mouth.

Cat closed her eyes, willing the image away, along with struggling to make her racing heart slow down.

"Who was that?"

"A woman I used to babysit for."

"You okay?"

Cat had babysat plenty of times with no issues until that one terrible day. She'd just earned her babysitter's certificate, having passed a CPR class with flying colors, yet none of it had helped in the end. She couldn't save that little girl.

"Yeah," she finally choked out. "Fine."

Simon gave her an encouraging squeeze as if he didn't quite believe her, but he didn't question her further.

Opal cooed and patted Cat's chest, almost as if she too knew how much it hurt seeing Sue Jensen.

Cat stared at the Center Park tree with its glowing multicolored lights. Snow fell and Cat tried to rally her spirits, but the pleasant moment had been tarnished. Reminded once again of how quickly lives could shatter with one careless action, Cat was determined to keep her past buried. Forever.

She'd finally faced the woman she'd feared seeing and Cat hadn't fallen apart. Time would never heal this wound, and she wasn't about to reopen it. There was no sense going back to it. Not ever.

Chapter Six

Simon followed Cat up the stairs to Zach and Ginger's expansive apartment above their blown-glass shop. If Christmas were a place, he'd say Maple Springs seemed close to it. The snow, the tree lighting and the smell of hot apple cider that emanated from the kitchen all reminded him of those seasonal commercials he'd seen on TV. Only this was real and the Zelinsky family had invited him to be part of their holiday.

Cat cast off her coat onto a bench and pulled the baby out of the wrap carrier. Even Opal had been dressed in a seasonal red, white and green romper with a reindeer face, complete with a fuzzy red ball for a nose. She looked like a Christmas present, a holiday baby.

Simon reached for his daughter, enormously pleased with the smile on her face. "Come here, Princess."

"She has a name, you know." Despite the scolding words, Cat gave him an indulgent look and shook her head as she pulled off the baby's hat and fleece mittens.

Simon cuddled the baby close, inhaling her soft, powdery scent. "Opal is a curious choice of name."

"An obvious one, considering—wait, don't you like it?" Cat slipped off the wrap carrier.

It warmed him to think that Cat had named their daughter after the very thing that had brought them together. "I like it very much. Does she have a middle name?"

"Elizabeth. Same as my mom's."

"Opal Elizabeth Roberts. Sounds regal, don't you think? Princess suits her."

"Yeah." Cat's gaze didn't quite meet his.

It dawned on him that he'd assumed she'd given Opal his name. Perhaps she hadn't. "It is Roberts, yes?"

Cat shook her head. "No. I gave her my last name."

"But the birth certificate—"

"You weren't there, and because we're not married, you weren't named."

Simon instinctively held Opal tighter. He had no legal claim on this baby—not according to the paperwork, anyway. No proof that she was even his. Or that he belonged to her.

"Glad you could make it, Simon. I can hold Opal if you two want to grab some snacks." Ginger held out her arms.

He didn't want to let his daughter go and hesitated, anger boiling up inside him. Finally, he handed the baby over, relieved that Opal settled comfortably into the crook of Ginger's arm without fussing. He glanced at Cat.

She looked miserable and fiddled with a button on the oversize black-and-red checked flannel shirt she wore over a white turtleneck and leggings. He watched her slip off the clunky black boots to reveal fuzzy socks sporting a Christmas-tree design.

So different from the sleek linen clothes she'd worn in Africa. She seemed different too, far less confident than before. What had he done over the four days they'd spent in the Ethiopian Highlands to make her think he wouldn't want to know that he had a daughter?

Ginger kept talking. "Are you going to stay open next Saturday night for the shoppers' walk?"

Simon nodded, his gaze never leaving Cat's face. "I'll be open."

"Great. Don't forget to decorate." Ginger grinned and took off with the baby.

"Simon, I…" Cat stopped.

What explanation could she possibly give that might make him feel better? He stared at her feet in an attempt to extinguish the inferno raging inside him. "I like your socks."

Her startled gaze finally flew to his. "They get me in the Christmas mood."

The inferno temporarily banked, Simon whispered, "Why didn't you tell me? I could have been there."

She tipped her head. "I didn't know where you were, or if you'd even care. I chose to handle this on my own."

"You didn't give me a choice."

Cat's face paled with guilt. The same expression she'd had when she'd bumped into that woman.

"Why did seeing that woman upset you?"

"Upset me? No, just surprised me." Cat's expression hardened. "Come on, let's get some cider."

He dropped the subject for now. "Lead the way."

"When should we decorate your shop?"

"We?"

Her eyes widened. "Oh, I'd assumed. Never mind. If you don't want to be involved, then I can take care of it."

That made him feel like a first-class heel. "How about this week?" Simon hung back from the table laden with holiday goodies and surrounded by other members of Cat's family. He wasn't in the mood to mingle.

Cat looked reluctant, as well. She reached into her

pocket and drew out the spare key to his house. "I forgot to give you this."

"Keep it."

Her eyes narrowed. "Why?"

"It just seems like a good idea."

Whosoever shall lose his life, shall preserve it.

That verse kept slipping into his thoughts. His old life was gone. He had a new life now, one in which he tried to keep God at the center. He thought he'd heard from God with that verse when it came to going back to hunting for gems. It was what he loved and he missed the adventure, but what if he'd interpreted it all wrong?

Sunday morning, Cat stood next to Simon. She'd promised her parents she'd go to a service somewhere, so here she was, at Simon's church. Her brothers' church too.

It was a pleasant place, with cushioned pews and bright blocks of stained glass at the top of the windows. Ginger was one of the singers up front with the band of musicians leading the song service.

She glanced at Simon, standing beside her, holding a sleeping Opal. He sang softly, but she could easily detect his deep, smooth voice among the others surrounding them.

They'd had an awkward evening at her brother's place that had ended with Simon leaving early. Not being listed as the father on Opal's birth certificate had clearly upset him. So much still lay unsettled between them.

He'd offered financial support, but so far, other than temporarily hiring her, he hadn't named an amount. Hadn't given her an hourly wage or salary figure either. She'd wanted to be independent, thinking she could raise Opal on her own. She was beginning to understand her dad's views. Cat needed help and Opal would need

Simon, but how did she make him see that his support needed to be more than money?

He leaned toward her. "Would you like to pick up decorations for the shop after church?"

"Where?"

"I understand there's a farmers market with fresh greenery not far from here."

She had the wrap carrier with her, so having the baby tag along would work. "I know where it is. Yes, I'm in."

Cat was looking forward to picking out wreaths and garlands. Christmas was an easy holiday to get lost in. For a few precious weeks, she could pretend all was well—as long as she ignored the fact that Christmas meant seeing the last of Simon for however long his assignment might be. One more thing they hadn't ironed out.

Simon caught her watching him and tipped his head in question, unconsciously adjusting Opal in his arms when she let out a little whine. The awkwardness he'd first shown at holding their daughter was gone.

Their daughter.

Her throat tightened and tears threatened.

He looked concerned. "What?"

She swallowed hard. "You hold her like a pro now."

"Thank you." He sat down and shifted Opal to his shoulder, but his frown deepened.

Cat sat too. She focused on the minister as he went over a list of announcements. She couldn't pay attention with Simon sitting close, distracting her with the gentle way he rubbed Opal's back.

When the minister began his message, though, Cat's ears perked up at the title. *Fight against letting the past dictate one's future.*

"You will never really believe God is enough, until God is all you have," the minister said.

Once again, Cat's mind went to questions she'd asked countless times before. God was all she'd had that day Muriel had drowned. Cat had prayed, begged, even screamed for His help. Why'd He let her die? Of course, she was well aware it was her fault, not God's. She'd been the one not paying attention. For all she knew, God had tried to get her attention and failed.

By the time church was over, Opal had fallen asleep on Simon's shoulder. Cat folded the fleece blanket that had been stuffed into the car seat. "You can put her in the seat."

"I don't want to wake her."

"You won't."

Simon hesitated only a moment before settling the baby into the car seat. He fastened the straps and then waited for Cat to slip on the fleece hat before he draped the blanket over Opal. "Ready?"

"Yup." She wanted out of this church with its message that made her think too much.

They exited the sanctuary, Simon nodding to folks who greeted him. He even waved at her brother Zach but kept walking.

"You can talk with these people if you want."

"Don't want to. We have things to do." He nodded for her to keep moving.

Simon wasn't a chatty guy. He'd been quiet at her parents' for Thanksgiving and even last night at Zach's. Back in Ethiopia, his reputation had been rock solid. Everyone agreed he knew his stuff. He was well trusted but wasn't very conversational. How did a man like that adjust to a child who needed ample stimulation and interaction? Opal might bring joy, but also complication. Simon seemed like he wanted to be a father, but he hadn't said how, other than financial support. Was he up to the challenge of truly being part of Opal's life? And how would Cat deal with it if he was?

Sitting together at church felt too much like they were together, a couple. They weren't anywhere near that. Simon hadn't made any moves toward her that way and that was fine by her. Sort of. Cat had never intended on getting married and having kids. Losing one or the other had always been too great a risk. Impossible dreams, considering her past.

They loaded the baby into Cat's car because Simon had walked to church. The farmers market was only a few miles away, so the drive wouldn't be long. It had snowed overnight, leaving behind a couple of inches on the ground. Every time the sun peeked through the clouds, it turned lawns into glimmering nets of white.

Cat couldn't take the silence stretching between them and racked her brain for an easy subject to discuss. Simon had lived in Maple Springs for half a year, yet he hadn't made any connections that she could see other than with her brother Zach. "How did you like living here?"

"Not enough to stay."

"Why's that?" Cat kept her eyes on the road. "What is it that you don't like?"

Simon shrugged. "It's not the town—it's me."

"Do you find it harder to get to know people here?" Cat dug deeper. "Other than Zach, have you made friends, you know, connections?"

He narrowed his eyes. "Is that your way of asking if I'm seeing someone?"

She hadn't meant it quite that way, but— "Are you?"

He chuckled. "No."

She tried again. "Actually, it's for a freelance piece about Maple Springs. I might as well keep my journalism going as much as I can, considering that managing your store might be temporary. I'd love insight from someone new to the area."

"Well, I've been welcomed into the community. Not only by your family, but others too. There's a storybook quality here."

"As in too good to be real?"

He laughed. "I was thinking more along the lines of insulated, but with the common goal of tourism. As a new business owner, everyone pushed for me to buy into that. I don't know. I simply wanted to try my hand at selling my own jewelry, not save the town."

Cat could imagine how it might have been. New businesses downtown were always a big deal. The shops were a big draw for tourists, so everyone wanted to weigh in on what each shop should offer. By the sounds of it, Simon hadn't wanted to be involved in the downtown merchant scene with chamber meetings and local politics. The man was an island, self-reliant and ready to ship out on adventures, leaving no ties behind.

They pulled into an already filled parking lot of the market. In the designated area, Christmas trees were lined up by size and type and price, along with a chipboard wall full of various sizes of wreaths.

Cat parked and got out. She quickly slipped out of her coat and pulled on the baby carrier so her hands would be free as she looked around. She gathered up a still-sleeping Opal and nestled her inside the wrap.

Opal fussed a little but settled back down with a sigh.

Cat reached for her coat, but Simon was there, holding it out for her. She slipped into each arm. "Thank you."

"Good idea, that thing." He pointed at the wrap.

"Yeah." Cat ignored the flip of her belly when Simon stepped closer to close the snaps on the front of her coat halfway up.

"Thank you for doing this." His deep voice caressed her ears. His dark eyes looked soft.

"It's what you hired me for, remember?"

His eyes clouded over. "About that, we need to discuss the terms of your employment, along with support for Opal."

"True, but not here. Not now." Cat wanted to enjoy this. Was it so bad to wish they were doing this simply to get into the season?

"Right you are. Perhaps after, we can grab some lunch."

"Deal."

They walked silently through the throngs of people checking out Christmas trees, and Cat found herself getting caught up in the holiday cheer. "I love decorating for Christmas. I don't go all out like my mom, but there's nothing quite like the smell of fresh pine." She pointed toward the wreaths. "Is this what you're looking for?"

He shrugged. "I guess. Red bows, pinecones. Nothing too elaborate. Traditional."

"Then this will be easy. Are you putting up a tree in your shop?"

"No. Too cluttered."

Cat laughed. "One tiny tree would be too cluttered? Man, you are sparse."

"That I am." He didn't join in her amusement.

Maybe she'd hit a nerve with that one statement. It sure seemed like Simon kept his life as bare as his rented house, swept clean and free of entanglements. That had changed with Opal. Now that he knew he was a father who hadn't been named on their baby's birth certificate, would he try to be free of her?

Simon peeked through his storefront window at Opal in her car seat, trying to grab the animal rattles over-

head that Cat had clipped on. Resisting the urge to go in
there and help her latch on to the toy, Simon watched for
a few more seconds.

She seemed happy enough, and even though he and
Cat were outside, hanging garland, they could clearly see
where the baby was situated inside, where it was nice and
warm. They'd hear her too, if she started to cry.

"Is she okay?" Cat stood on the ladder, adjusting the
garland. According to her, he'd hung it lopsided.

"Yes. She can't quite reach those rattles, but she seems
to be enjoying the challenge." Simon smiled up at her.

She wore that big puffy coat, along with a bright red
knit hat and leather work gloves. Snow fell softly from the
sky, sticking in her hair as it landed. She looked beautiful
and he didn't quite know what to do about that.

She climbed down from the ladder. "Where do you
want the wreaths?"

He didn't care about wreaths.

"Simon?"

He snapped out of it and stepped back, looking over
the pine garland twined with cedar and pinecones. That
fresh evergreen and pine-sap smell stuck to both him and
Cat. He liked it. "Three wreaths across the top, where the
garland is affixed, don't you think?"

Cat studied the storefront. "Yes, that would look nice
and then you'd still have the fourth wreath for the door. I
need to fill the window box with more greenery, though."

"Where will you get that?" Simon climbed up the ladder before he gave in to the urge to pull Cat close enough
to see if she smelled as good as all this pine and snow.

She handed him one of the wreaths. "I can cut a bunch
of pine boughs and evergreen and even some small birch
branches in the woods behind my parents' place."

"Perhaps we should do that together, as well. Sounds

like a big job." He didn't like the idea of her out in the woods, alone, cutting down things.

He affixed the fragrant balsam wreath on the nail that held up the garland, pleased with the long tails from the red velvet bow. Cat had insisted on buying plenty of ribbon at the market, and she'd been right.

"Your help would be welcome. We're going to need a lot to fill this in."

The window box ran the length of the window at sidewalk level. "I could hire the same people who filled it with flowers for the summer."

Cat shook her head. "Too costly, plus it will be fun to do it ourselves. Since you're not getting a tree, I thought maybe a big vase of pine and evergreen on the counter would bring a little Christmas inside."

"Hmm." She was bringing a little Christmas into everything.

He'd never celebrated the holidays. Never had a reason to, or anyone he'd wanted to share them with. He wondered what this Christmas might provide. Most likely a repeat of Thanksgiving at the Zelinsky house, and that didn't quite do it for him.

"What about lights?" Cat handed him another wreath.

"I want to keep it simple. I have the window lit from inside."

Cat peered in the window at the baby.

He did too. Opal had her whole fist in her mouth. "Is that normal?"

"She's been doing that a lot lately. I don't know, maybe she's hungry."

The image of Cat in his rocking chair, wistfully staring out the window as she fed Opal, hit him, filling him with longing. The scene changed to the three of them in his home for Christmas, with simple decorations and a fire and happiness. The image sliced through him with uncomfortable clarity. Maybe it could happen…but he was sure it couldn't last. He'd mess that picture up eventually. Better not to risk it.

Simon quickly moved the ladder, trying to erase the lingering images. "She's not the only one. Let's finish up here, and I'll purchase a couple sandwiches at the place across the street. What would you like?"

Cat hung the final wreath on the door and fiddled with the ribbon. "It doesn't matter, anything with turkey will do."

He climbed down, folded the ladder and leaned it against the wall. Taking in his storefront, he saw that Cat was right about the empty window box looking, well, empty. But the garlands and wreaths set off the store nicely without looking cluttered. "This looks good."

"It will look even better when that window box is full."

"Quite so." He nodded.

This reminded him of that one Christmas in London when the master jeweler he'd apprenticed under had invited him to spend the holiday at his home. The man's wife and daughters had stuffed pine and boxwood and holly everywhere. They'd given him gifts too, in an attempt to make him feel like part of their family. He'd felt out of place with nothing to give in return.

He'd buried warm feelings of hearth and home so deep, it hurt when they resurfaced. He'd never had a normal family life, but if the truth were told, he'd always wanted one. He'd tried to provide some stability for his siblings, but it had fallen apart fast. He'd failed them, just like he'd fail Opal.

He glanced at Cat and his gut twisted. He'd fail her too. She smiled at him. "We could gather those greens at my parents' tomorrow if you don't have other plans."

"No plans."

A bald-faced lie. He'd always planned to steer clear of deep connections in his life. Stepping into family life put him in way over his head. Deep enough to drown, for sure.

Cat finished feeding Opal and then shifted to pat the baby's back. She heard Simon return with their lunch. "We're back here."

Simon entered the workshop area and set a big paper bag on a small table.

Cat shifted Opal to her other shoulder. "She took a bottle for a little bit today."

Simon's brows drew into a frown, but he didn't say a word. The tension over that development book's recommendations still hung between them.

Cat needed to make her return to work a smooth transition. Simon had voiced his disapproval in her bringing Opal to work. Once he was gone, depending on customer traffic patterns, she might be able to swing it some days. But at least some days, Opal would be home with Cat's mother, and she needed to be able to eat.

When he still didn't speak, she pushed a little harder. "I have to get her used to a bottle. I don't want to leave my mom with a cranky baby."

His frown deepened as he emptied the contents of the bag. "I got you a turkey club."

The change of subject wasn't lost on her. He still disapproved. "Thank you."

Opal burped. Loud.

It made Cat chuckle.

Simon smiled as well but suddenly gathered up the sandwiches and placed them back in the bag. "It's too cold in here. Why don't we have lunch at my house, where we can build a fire? I have something for Opal."

"You do?" Cat tipped her head. "What is it?"

"A baby swing."

Cat stared at him.

He quickly looked away. "So there's a third choice between car seat and floor."

"That's wonderful. Thanks."

Simon looked uncomfortable with her gratitude. "Let's go."

She gathered up her things and bundled Opal back in the car seat while Simon turned off the lights and placed the ladder inside.

He held the door open for her.

"Thank you."

He gave her a hint of a smile as he set the alarm and locked the door. "Sure thing."

Could Simon be a sure thing for her and Opal? Babies came with a lot of clutter that would challenge his decluttered world. Yet he'd purchased a swing for Opal and that development book. He was trying.

Less than ten minutes later, Cat pulled into Simon's driveway. When they got out, the snow that had been light had turned a little heavier, blanketing the ground with a hushed crumpling sound as the thick flakes hit piles of dried leaves. "This looks like it'll stay."

"You think so?" Simon held open the door to his rental.

Cat nodded. "It's pretty, don't you think? The snow. It doesn't get all dirty like in the city."

"True." Simon set the brown bag with their lunch on the table. "I'll get a fire started."

Cat sat on the plush living room rug. She spread out the fleece blanket and placed Opal on her belly, since she hadn't fallen asleep on the way over. The baby gurgled and cooed and kicked her legs.

Cat glanced at Simon, crouched in front of the fireplace, stacking sticks and kindling. Even the way he built a fire was neat and tidy. He didn't toss the small sticks in a pile but stacked them carefully before using a long fireplace match that he touched to the kindling. The wood caught quickly, snapping and crackling.

Opal squealed, drawing Simon's startled gaze.

Cat laughed. "I think she likes your fireplace."

"Look but don't touch, Opal."

Her heart warmed at his firm voice. He was serious about keeping her safe and that was sweet. It'd be months before Opal could crawl close to the hearth. Chances were they wouldn't be here then. Her mood took a sharp nosedive. Getting to know Simon a little more, she didn't want him to up and leave and that wasn't only for Opal's sake. Cat realized she'd miss him too.

"I'll get that swing so we can eat." Simon stepped down the hall, returning with a very solid, safe baby swing.

Cat hadn't moved. She watched as he placed the swing near the table. She knew the model because she'd researched them all. "When did you do this?"

"Last night, after I left Zach's."

Had he gone all the way to the next town over simply for this? "It's a good one, Simon. Thank you."

"No problem. I figured that it might be helpful when you're here." Again he looked away as if uncomfortable with her thanks. "Come on, let's eat."

She got up with Opal, settled her into the swing and secured the strap with a soft click. Simon tossed a couple more logs onto the now blazing fire. She joined him at the table with one glance back at Opal, who was staring at the dangling yellow plush flower rattles overhead. The baby kicked and reach for the flowers and missed.

"Soft drink?" Simon held up two different cans of pop; both were without caffeine. Probably due to more reading of that development book. Another hit to her heart. He was definitely trying.

"I'm fine with either one, so you choose."

He took the ginger ale and offered her the root beer. Then he bowed his head, but he didn't pray aloud. In seconds, he was done.

Cat wasn't sure what to make of this praying Simon. She often found it hard to pray because she didn't think she should approach God with the small stuff. He had bigger concerns to deal with and yet even prayers for big stuff seemed like she overstepped her bounds. Cat didn't believe she deserved answered prayers.

She closed her eyes for a second and sighed. "I love how quiet it is here."

Simon looked up from unwrapping his sandwich. "Neighbors aren't too close. Summertime you can hear the road more with the windows open."

"Still, it's nothing like New York or my parents' house. My little sister Erin moved back in and soon my brother Luke will be home from college for Christmas break. Between the TV and radio and everyone—" Cat shook her head. "I'm too used to having my own place."

He looked at her. Through her. "I've been thinking about how to best support you and Opal. What if you moved in here after I'm gone? I have a lease until May. That way, I'll have a place to store my things, and you'll have your own space."

Tempting. She liked this house. There was the view and the quiet and— "What about when you come back?"

"That depends."

"On what?"

"You."

Cat's stomach flipped. "Me? How?"

His dark eyes suddenly looked merry. "Your sales."

"But managing your jewelry store is only temporary, even after my trial period."

He leaned back. "I'm rethinking that."

Cat gripped her sandwich so hard, the avocado slipped out from under the bun. "What about gem hunting?"

"I'm not giving that up. I like the idea of purchasing my own gems too much. Besides, working with investors to find theirs will partially fund mine with travel expenses at least. I decided not to break my lease early, so I'll have more time to figure it out. Having you manage the store might work perfectly."

Even if it was only until the end of May, five months of peace and quiet might be worth it. Surely he wouldn't be gone that long? She could always head back to her parents' house when needed. Keeping his shop open meant sales. The more jewelry she sold, the more he'd have to replace. The sooner he'd have to return. "What about inventory? Do you have enough stock to last through May?"

He shrugged. "I have a month to make more."

She smothered the urge to smile. "Let's talk salary."

Simon's eyes gleamed with approval. "Very well, Catherine, let's do that."

The sound of her given name spoken with that buttery voice of his sent a tremor through her. Something was happening between them. As if that connection they'd had when they'd first met was rewiring itself, trying to fire up and pulse with new energy. Should she spur the process or pull the plug?

As tempting as the idea was, pursuing a romantic relationship with Simon wasn't something to be taken lightly.

They had Opal to consider, which meant they'd always have a relationship. She'd prefer it to be a friendly one. Cat wasn't ready for better or worse.

Or was she?

Simon itched for gem hunting and that wouldn't change. He'd be away more than he'd be home. Could he even commit for the long haul? Could she? It was much too soon to tell.

Chapter Seven

Monday morning, Simon stared out the window as he made tea. It had snowed more overnight, leaving mounds of the fluffy white stuff piled in his driveway. He should shovel before going anywhere.

Cat thought snow was pretty and that made him smile.

She and Opal had stayed only for a bit after lunch and his place seemed terribly empty after they'd left. That emptiness still hung in the air. He didn't know what had possessed him to offer her this little rental for her and Opal to live. Hearing her complaints about her parents' home resonated. He didn't care to hang out there either.

It certainly stalled his plans to cut ties to Maple Springs, but he had some breathing room. Six months to reconsider leaving or following through. A lot depended on Cat and her abilities with the shop. A lot depended on what she wanted from him.

She hadn't once pushed for support, making him believe what she'd told him when they'd run into each other at church. She wanted nothing from him—other than a job.

Opal was young. If he left her behind in six months, she wouldn't miss him, would she? What if he missed her?

Gathering up his insulated mug of tea, Simon pushed

all thoughts of wanting and missing aside. Those desires led to disappointment. He was good at taking care of himself, but not other people.

He headed for the door and a morning spent with Cat gathering greens from the woods on her parents' property. He'd always been one for a treasure hunt and this might turn into one. He threw a couple of large laundry baskets in the back of his car, hoping they'd find enough for the window box in front of his shop.

The better he knew Cat, the more confident he'd feel leaving his shop in her hands. She'd done well with the customer looking for something less expensive, but Simon needed to see how Cat did with the other customers across the spectrum. He'd had some high-end sales since opening his doors here.

When he pulled into the Zelinsky driveway, Simon thought the snow cover made the lawn look even more expansive. Cat's parents were outside, hooking up an extension cord to lighted deer figures. Made out of twisted wood, the deer were garnished with fresh greenery and large red bows tied around their necks. Evergreen garlands hung along the roof of the front porch and two wreaths graced the skinny windows on either side of the front door. The house looked like something he'd see on a Christmas card. Warm and inviting.

An image of Opal as a toddler on this lawn, bundled in a snowsuit and playing with her grandparents, suddenly flashed in his mind. Opal belonged here, in this town, with her grandparents nearby. He'd never known his grandparents.

"Hi, Simon." Helen waved him in. "Go on inside. Cat's waiting for you."

"Thank you." He gave Cat's father a nod, grateful the man gave him a friendly nod in return.

As he stepped inside the house, the deep bass beat of a stereo playing upstairs hit him first, the television second and then a gasp, followed by a baby's ear-splitting cry. *Opal.*

Then Cat's frantic voice. "Erin, get Mom!"

Cat's sister ran by him, flinging open the door and yelling for their mom to come quick.

Simon rushed into the living room. "What happened?"

Cat looked up, her face pasty white. She held a howling Opal, rocking her back and forth. "She rolled off the couch."

Simon drew closer and knelt down. "Let me see."

"No." Cat tightened her hold.

"Cat—" he gently coaxed. He didn't like the wild look in her eyes.

"What happened?" Helen came in, followed by Cat's father. She immediately reached for Opal, whose cries had quieted to a mewling whimper.

Was that a good sign or bad? Simon didn't know and looked at Helen to find out. She seemed calm in the face of Cat's terror.

After handing over the baby to her mom, Cat pulled her legs up to her chest and kept rocking. "I was changing her and reached for the powder from the diaper bag and down she went."

Helen laid Opal on another couch and checked her over, gently shushing the baby. "There there, Opal. You're okay."

Opal did indeed look uninjured as she kicked her legs and reached with her arms.

Simon glanced at Cat. She still teetered like a woman gone mad. He took in the surroundings. Powder sprinkles smeared across a square mat draped on the couch.

A rolled-up diaper lay on the floor, next to a thick fuzzy blanket. "Cat, where did she hit?"

She looked at him as if he'd asked the color of the moon.

He grasped her sock-covered feet to stop her from rocking. "Did she land on the blanket?"

Cat sniffed, rallying. "I think so, yeah."

Simon relaxed even more when Opal cooed.

"She's fine, Cat. Just got scared." Helen stood, holding a bare-bottomed Opal in her arms.

Opal gurgled and then squealed, sounding every bit recovered from her tumble.

Simon wanted to reach for the baby but knew Cat needed him more when she crumpled into the couch, her eyes filling with new tears. He sat next to her and gathered her hands in his, giving her fingers a gentle shake. "Hey—"

"Grab the diaper bag, Andy. Relax, Cat, I'll finish changing her upstairs and bring her back down." Helen gave Simon an encouraging smile and then breezed out of the room.

Cat's father and sister followed.

With everyone gone, Cat looked more composed, but still shaken. "I'm sorry, I should be the one tending to Opal's needs right now."

"Let your mom do this for you." Simon didn't know the first thing about taking care of their daughter's possible bump or bruise. He was glad Helen Zelinsky had far more experience with this sort of thing than him.

"What kind of terrible mother lets her ten-week-old baby roll off the couch?"

"Stop." Simon squeezed her hands, glad that she didn't pull away from him. "This could have happened to anyone. It could have just as easily been me. Then you'd never let me change her again."

That earned him a slight smile, exactly what he'd been aiming for. It looked like this had really rattled her. Honestly, her reaction seemed a bit much. But then, what did he know?

She pinned him with a direct stare. "You really want to change her?"

Did he? Simon backtracked and looked away. "Not exactly something I look forward to doing…"

Cat pulled away and stood. "I'm going to check on her."

Simon watched Cat leave and then stood and slipped out of his wool coat, draping it across the rocker. He noticed that the music upstairs had stopped. A cheerful fire blazed in the hearth and open boxes of Christmas decorations graced the hardwood floor.

Fortunately, Opal had not only rolled onto a soft blanket, but one that lay atop a thick area rug. Despite the harmless outcome, Simon knew how quickly accidents could happen with wee ones.

When he was twelve, his five-year-old sister had slipped and hit her head on the corner of the kitchen table while they'd been playing tag. As if that hadn't been bad enough, his mother asked the guy down the hall of their apartment building to do a stitch job, which was so sloppy it left a zigzag of a scar on her forehead.

His mother had refused to go to the ER because of the money. Simon had been furious, but there wasn't much he could do other than try to talk some sense into her. He remembered how his mother yelled back that until he found a job, he could keep his mouth shut. He didn't, though. He'd muttered that she managed to find money for drugs and booze, and that had earned him a slap across the face.

He'd wanted to run away back then but knew he needed to look after his little sister and brother. Noble for a preteen, but when it counted, he hadn't been there for them. After he'd been kicked out, he'd run away from his responsibility to them. Was he doing the same thing now?

No. This was different.

Cat returned with a newly changed Opal, shutting down his thoughts. She looked more composed.

He reached for his daughter, relieved when Cat handed her over. Searching Opal's face, he didn't see any swollen bumps or lumps. Not even a scratch.

Opal stretched her little hand toward his face, missing his nose.

He blew noisy kisses into the palm of Opal's hand, enjoying the baby smiles he received in return. "We don't have to get those greens today."

"Yes, we do. My mom will watch the baby." Cat looked determined.

"You okay?" What he'd perceived a moment ago as calm now looked like holding it together. Barely. Cat seemed too upset for a simple tumble, so he prodded. "Tell me."

Her eyes darkened and she blinked rapidly, but she didn't speak. Finally, she sighed with a shrug. "It scared me, is all."

Simon knew purposeful distancing when he saw it. He'd practiced the art of deflection his whole life. He'd let it go for now—would wait to bring it up again when they were alone rather than in a house full of people. "Opal's our first. Everything's scary."

Her eyes grew round.

That had come out wrong. He hadn't meant to imply

that they'd have more babies. Cutting through the awkward silence, Simon got back to the reason he'd come. "How do you want to do this with the greens? I only brought a couple laundry baskets with me."

She looked relieved at the change of subject. "We have stuff. I think snowshoes would work well too."

"What?"

Cat gave him a weak smile. "You'll see."

After making sure Opal was okay, after feeding her again to be certain, Cat had finally suited up for their outdoor trek. She demonstrated how to walk in snowshoes on the front lawn. Her parents had several pairs in different sizes, so she'd easily found a set to fit Simon.

"Do we really need these?" He lifted his foot. He'd caught on quickly, not that it was terribly difficult.

"There's a good eight inches or more on the ground in places with higher drifts. Trust me, you'll be glad we have them after walking a ways." She pulled a deep plastic sled her father used for ice fishing behind her, loaded with tree loppers and a couple of pairs of pruning shears.

"Lead on." Simon walked next to her.

The shushing rhythm of the metal snowshoes seemed loud against their silence. Even worse was Simon's nervous expression when he'd looked at her—

"Do you want to talk about it? You were pretty upset."

"No, I'm okay." She wasn't.

She'd freaked out over Opal falling to the floor. It had happened so fast. Cat wouldn't soon forget the horrifying sound of Opal hitting the floor with a thud. It didn't matter that the floor was carpeted or that the blanket had helped soften the fall even further; the problem was still that Cat had looked away. She'd been fiddling with the diaper bag zipper, trying to close it after pulling out the powder.

When she'd finally gone upstairs to check on her daughter, Cat's mom had scolded her good. Not for letting Opal fall, but for thinking she was a terrible mother because of it. Cat wanted to believe her mother, but how could she not think about the day the Jensen girl fell off the dock into the lake and drowned. Cat hadn't been paying close enough attention then either.

Glancing at him and the smooth way he moved through the snow, she took a deep breath. "Thank you for, I don't know, being there for me. It did shake me up some."

His expression softened. "You're welcome."

They made it to the edge of the woods and Simon unwrapped his scarf. He didn't wear a hat.

Cat smiled. "It's a workout, huh?"

He smiled back. "It is."

"But easier than walking a long way in this much snow without the snowshoes." Cat followed the edge of mainly hardwoods for a few feet until she found the path. "This way."

Again, they walked in silence, until Cat stopped at a grove of pines. "Here. I think a bunch of these boughs will make a good base. Farther on toward the lake, where it's marshier, there are cedars and small birch trees. I think we can fill in holes with clippings of those."

"Sounds good." Simon grabbed the loppers and started cutting the lower branches.

Cat used the pruning shears to clip smaller ones. She snipped pinecones too. They'd look pretty tucked in with the birch branches. It didn't take long to fill up the deep plastic sled. Simon took over pulling it as they ventured closer toward the lake.

Sparse snowflakes drifted from the sky, scattering

over them only to melt after landing. Cat breathed the fresh air in deep. "It's nice out here, quiet."

"Almost too quiet," Simon said. "Like I shouldn't disrupt it by talking."

"Yeah." Cat nodded, relieved that it wasn't her or what had happened with Opal that had kept Simon from speaking much.

He made his way toward a young birch tree and looked up.

Cat looked up too. "If we can get a few of those thinner branches above, they'd look really nice in the window box."

"A little high." Just out of Simon's reach.

Cat looked at him. "Can you lift me?"

"I believe I can." He grinned.

Her breath caught. She loved the way Simon smiled. With that teasing grin, he looked even more handsome.

He stepped close. "Ready?"

She nodded, her heart lodged in her throat at his nearness.

Simon lifted her, but she wobbled, making him unsteady too. "Put your hands on my shoulders."

She did so, but it was too late. The only way they could keep from falling was to put her back on the ground. He loosened his hold and she slid down the front of him until they were face-to-face. She trembled.

"Are you cold?" Simon tightened his arms around her, his dark eyes piercing. Magnetic.

She wasn't the least bit cold. He was only a breath away.

It would be so easy to kiss him. Easy to test his response and see if it was as strong as before, when they'd been in that hut. She wanted to, but he was leaving for who knew how long—and she wasn't sure she could count on him to come back. Not for good. "This isn't going to work."

Simon's nose touched hers. "No. Of course not."

He didn't have to agree with her so quickly. But while it stung her pride, she knew they were both making the rational decision. Some people were not meant to settle down and have families. Cat had considered herself among them because of her past, but now that she had Opal, she'd do the best she could to provide a stable life for her. Neither of them needed Simon popping in and out of their lives.

He'd settled in Maple Springs for six months, started a lucrative business and found that he didn't like it. The only reason he'd stalled closing up his shop was to give her a job. She'd pressed him on that too, knowing that he looked at providing for Opal as simply financial in nature.

Cat pulled away. "It might work better if I were on your shoulders."

He nodded, his expression closed. "Take those snow-shoes off and I'll give it a go."

After a couple of laughable tries, Cat finally made it onto his shoulders. Tucking her feet on either side of him for leverage, she reached for the tree loppers that Simon handed her. She made fast work of clipping several skinny and a few thicker birch branches.

"Done?"

"Yes." Cat handed back the loppers.

Simon tossed them on top of the pine and birch they'd gathered and then backed against a tree. Grasping her mitten-covered hands in his, he bent so she could slip off him. She did, losing one mitten in the process.

Back on the ground, Cat picked it up and turned. "All we need now is cedar."

Simon's hair stuck up in places with static. "Lead the way."

Cat stared a moment before bending down to slip back into her snowshoes. Her fingers shook at the emotions coursing through her. These feelings of neediness nearly overwhelmed her.

Despite his painful upbringing, she believed he could be a good father. Proving that was bound to place Cat in a precarious position, one that might engage her heart. Showing Simon that Opal needed him might reveal that she needed him too, and then what?

What if Simon didn't want them and left anyway? What then?

After gathering the cedar clippings, Simon followed Cat back to the house. He rebuked himself for coming much too close to kissing Cat. He couldn't offer her a romantic relationship when he had no idea what one was even supposed to look like. He was no more suited to be a husband than he was a father.

They stopped at the driveway, near his Jeep. Each of them slipped out of the snowshoes.

Simon reached for the sled to load the greens into the back of his car when he noticed Cat pulling the birch twigs out of the pile, along with the pinecones. "What are you doing?"

"I need to glue the pinecones onto sticks and I want to jazz up the birch twigs a little."

"Jazz up?" Simon had no idea what she was talking about.

"Spray some glittery stuff on them so they'll pop."

He wasn't sure he liked the sound of that. "Glitter?"

She patted his arm. "Not what you're thinking. Nothing gaudy, I promise. I'll bring them tomorrow so you'll see before I stick them in there. What time do you want me at your store?"

Simon stared at her. He was still getting his bearings after holding her close. But he knew she was right to force his thoughts back to business. He'd hired her to manage his shop while he was gone and needed to show her what to do. He needed to concentrate on making enough inventory for the next five months. "How about one?"

Cat nodded. "Sounds good. My mom has already agreed to watch Opal."

"You can bring her."

Cat looked confused. Attractively so. "But I thought you said—"

He stopped her with a raised hand. "It shouldn't be too busy, and with both of us there, I can always take care of the customer if you're occupied with the baby."

Having Opal along would remind him of his responsibility, and hopefully keep him busy in the back, away from the temptation that was Cat.

Cat looked surprised, but pleased, and smiled. "Okay. One o'clock it is and we'll both be there."

Simon loaded up the rest of the greens.

Cat helped, putting her close to him again. "Would you like to come in for lunch?"

He was about to refuse, when his stomach growled loud enough for her to hear.

Cat laughed and tugged on his arm. "Come on."

He was hungry, but a sinking feeling told him that food wouldn't exactly satisfy. Still, he followed her into the house. He didn't like this itchy feeling around Cat. She might as well be a sprung trap waiting. If he didn't watch out where he stepped, she might sink her steel jaws of warm home and family into him.

Simon wasn't that sort of man. He had all his life up

to this point to prove that. If Cat started relying on him, he'd only let her down.

Entering the Zelinsky home, he cringed at the sound of Opal's howling cry. He'd heard that cry before, the day they'd first met.

Cat hurried to take their daughter from her mom. "Did you give her a bottle?"

"I tried, but she wasn't having any of it," Helen said. "Here, give me your coat."

Cat slipped out of her lightweight ski jacket as she shushed and rocked the baby. She grabbed the bottle from the counter and gave it a try. "Here you go, Opal."

The baby latched on but then promptly pushed away, crying with renewed vigor.

"Oh, Cat, give it up for now. Switching to a bottle takes time and you can't rush it."

"Not helping, Mom." Cat slipped out of the room in a huff.

Simon didn't dare comment, even though the words *I told you so* filtered through his thoughts. It had said as much in the book he'd purchased with hopes of gaining insight into babies.

He looked at Cat's father, who shrugged. "Would you like some lunch? Helen made white chili. We were about to have some."

Simon knew better than to refuse, now that he was inside. Besides, it smelled terribly good. "Yes. Thank you."

Andy Zelinsky grabbed bowls from the cupboard and placed them on a plate. He scooped a generous portion into each and then—after checking with Simon—topped it with shredded cheese. "Corn bread?"

Simon nodded. "Definitely."

Andy sort of smiled. "There's pop in the fridge."

Simon made himself at home, reaching for a can of soda and offering one to Cat's father.

"I've got water, but thank you. Have a seat."

He slipped into a chair across from Cat's dad, who bowed his head. Simon did so, as well.

"It doesn't get any easier," Andy said.

"What's that, sir?"

"Raising kids."

"You had ten." Simon couldn't keep the amazement out of his voice.

"Yes." No other explanation or reason given. "Cat tells us that you've hired her to manage your shop."

Simon felt the weight of Andy Zelinsky's disapproving gaze. "That's right, but I will help support Opal."

"Hmm. I suppose that's a start." Cat's father pushed a pad of paper and pen toward him. "I often have breakfast in town at Cam's diner. If you'll give me your number, I'd like to meet you there one day."

That was definitely stronger than a suggestion. He supposed he owed the man some time over breakfast, all things considered. Simon quickly jotted down his cell. "Might I have yours, as well?"

Andy Zelinsky showed only a trace of surprise.

"Just in case." Simon could think of any number of reasons he might need to get in touch with Cat's family. Her father's contact information was a good one to have tucked away in case of an emergency.

Andy wrote down his number and Helen's too and then ripped the sheet of paper off and handed it to him.

Simon was about to respond, but Cat entered with a baby monitor in hand. "Everything okay?" he asked.

Cat raised the monitor. "She's asleep."

She looked tired too. Would running the shop be too much for her? He'd find out soon enough, he supposed.

He tucked the paper in his pocket and turned his attention back to his bowl of white chili. He noticed a new tension in the room that wasn't there before. Perhaps Andy Zelinsky didn't approve of him—or of Cat working for him. Well, it might serve both their needs and it enabled him to support them. Cat hadn't yet mentioned what she'd expect for child support, so he'd offered her a rather generous salary.

The next step was finding out how they'd work together and, more important, how well she'd run his shop.

Chapter Eight

The next day, Simon spotted Cat through his storefront window wearing that festive red knit hat. He met her at the door. "Hello."

"Hey. Can you keep an eye on Opal for a minute? I brought the pinecones and birch for the window box."

"Sure." He took a sleeping Opal, bundled in her car seat, and set her on a bench behind the cash register, where it was nice and warm.

Sunshine streamed in through the door and window, warming his retail space even more. He could see Cat moving around outside, arranging branches amid the greenery he'd stuffed there yesterday. She placed pinecones that were attached to sticks within the clumps of pine and cedar branches.

It didn't take long before Cat peeked her head inside the store. "I'm done if you want to come out and see."

He checked to make sure that Opal was still asleep before following Cat outside. Glancing at the window box that ran the length of his storefront window, he liked what he saw. "Really nice."

She gave him a playful shove. "Come now, it's better than nice. I told you the glitter would work."

It did. She'd stuck red berries in with the pine alongside the birch and pinecones. The jazzed-up birch branches were coated in what looked like large sugary granules that shimmered in the light. She'd even twirled red velvet ribbon throughout the arrangement. "You were right. The storefront looks great with all this. Thank you."

She smiled. "Thank you for offering me a job."

His stomach took a dip, so he quickly checked his watch. Five long hours before he closed up shop. "Let's get started, then. I'll show you how the register works and all that goes with it."

"Sounds good." Cat entered the store and checked on Opal. "I have one more thing to grab from my car. Do you mind?"

"Not at all. Go ahead." Simon stood near the sleeping baby while Cat disappeared around the corner. Opal might not make as good a chaperone as he'd originally thought, considering the amount of time the baby slept.

Cat returned with a duffel bag.

"What's that?"

"A portable play-crib thing. I can't keep Opal in her car seat all afternoon. Where would you like me to put it?"

Babies came with all sorts of accessories. "How big is it?"

Cat pulled it from the duffel and popped it up in no time, adding a sort of shelf that was about halfway deep that turned it into a crib.

"Let's put it behind the counter, in the corner. It's warm there and she'll be out of the way, but you can still keep an eye on her throughout the store."

Cat smiled again. "Thank you for letting me bring her. I don't think she'll make any trouble. Overall, she's pretty good."

Until she screamed to be fed or needed changed. Even

then, Cat could use the back for privacy and he could cover the store. "No problem. I like seeing her."

Cat tipped her head as if she'd say something, but then didn't. Cat lifted Opal out of the car seat, wrapped her in a blanket and settled the baby on her back in the portable crib.

Opal barely stirred.

Cat slipped out of her coat and hung it on the rack next to his. "Okay, I'm ready."

Taking in how pretty she looked in the soft blue sweater she wore over black pants, he wasn't sure he was ready for any of this. "Let's start with the cash register. It's tablet based and pretty easy to use. Swipe credit cards here, accept cash there with an easy balance screen when we close. Everything is linked to my business software. Everything that happens here, I can check on through my laptop or phone. It's quite convenient."

Cat moved close as he showed her how it worked. Catching a whiff of her soft perfume, Simon stammered, "Yes, well, I forgot what I was saying."

"Printing a receipt."

"Right." Simon continued on.

"I think I have it. What's next?"

"The jewelry, everything here, plus I'm working on more. Although, I'm only doing custom orders for pickup by Christmas. Nothing after that." Simon scratched his forehead. "Any resizing on rings will be an issue. Perhaps I can find another jeweler not too far away we can partner with for repairs while I'm gone."

Cat nodded.

He showed Cat the back area with a small table and a mini fridge under a tiny counter, complete with a sink, coffee maker and electric teakettle. "The washroom is through there."

"Got it."

He nodded. "Very well, I've got a few pieces to finish up."

"Anything with those Welo opals?"

"Nothing yet."

Cat made a face. "Too bad. I'd love to see an end product, considering I was there when they came out of the mines."

"We'll see."

The bell on his door rang, announcing someone had come in. With a wiggle of her eyebrows, Cat welcomed them in and offered her assistance. She seemed very comfortable out there, even glancing toward Opal every so often.

This might work out well. For both of them.

By the end of the day, Cat had waited on several customers, successfully selling a pair of star sapphire earrings with a matching bracelet and an amazingly expensive chunky gold necklace with a large aquamarine pendant. Not bad for her first day. Even Simon had agreed.

She glanced at Opal, awake and reaching for the mobile overhead. Cat picked Opal up and made her way toward the back workshop to see what Simon was up to. He'd spent the better part of the afternoon holed up back there.

Opal cooed and kicked her legs when she spotted Simon.

Simon looked up and smiled. "It was a good day today."

"I think so." She leaned in for a look. "Is that an opal?"

"One of the smaller ones. What do you think?"

Cat watched the shimmers of color flash as he turned

the smooth side of the stone. Red and green and yellow amid blue fire. "It's gorgeous."

"Not even the most valuable one either. Would you pair it with silver or gold?"

"I prefer silver, but you're the expert. What goes better with opal?"

Simon smiled. "It's a matter of individual preference."

Cat tipped her head. "Do you ever wear anything you've made?"

He shrugged. "I pretty much stick with a watch."

"No men's jewelry?"

"Not yet. Something to consider, I suppose."

"Definitely."

"I'm thinking of grabbing a pizza for dinner. Do you want to join me?"

"I'll never turn down pizza." Cat grinned. "I like anything or everything on it."

Simon clicked off the grinding wheel. "Why don't you head for my place and I'll finish up here? You still have the key?"

"I do. I'll see you later, then." Cat gathered up her things, deciding to leave the portable crib. The baby had been great, very little fussing except when she was hungry, and the customers had loved her.

By the time she entered Simon's house and flicked on the light, she was ravenous. She'd eaten lunch before arriving at the jewelry shop but hadn't had anything since. She spread the fleece blanket on the living room carpet and laid Opal on her belly before going about the task of building a fire.

Opal kicked and squealed as Cat stacked kindling and lit the match. Staring into the flames, she heard the door open and turned.

Simon entered with a large pizza box and a foam container on top. "Thank you for starting the fire."

"You're welcome." Cat took the boxes from him so he could slip out of his coat. "Thanks for this. Pizza might be my favorite food, especially from here."

"I'll remember that." He looked around. "There's Opal. Hello, Princess."

Cat set the boxes on the counter and then turned to face him.

Simon looked at her. "What do you think about making over that second bedroom for her?"

Cat sucked in her breath. "Now?"

"I don't see why not. I ordered a crib and changing table from the same guy who made the rocker." Simon grabbed plates and set them on the table.

"That's generous of you." She didn't understand where he was coming from, giving her a job, his house, now a handmade crib for Opal.

"Cat, I might not know how to be a father, but I still want to provide for her. For you too. It's the right thing to do."

She wasn't keen on being viewed as a duty and stifled the urge to refuse. She blew out the breath she'd held instead. "Why don't we eat first, then discuss it?"

"What's to discuss?"

She watched as he grabbed a couple of cans of pop from the fridge. He handed one to her and then opened the box. The smell of cheesy pizza covered with pepperoni should have made her mouth water. Then he opened the smaller container, which held a side of wings with celery and blue cheese dressing.

"Catherine?"

She looked at him.

"Are you going to sit down?" His voice was soft but firm.

She slipped into a seat.

He offered her his hand. "Can we pray?"

She didn't feel like it but nodded. "You go ahead."

He bowed his head, asking God to bless the food and bless them, and that was it. Nothing about wisdom in this situation like before. Evidently, Simon had it all figured out. He thought she'd fall in with his plans so he could go on his merry way, feeling he'd done right by her and Opal.

"There's more to providing for a child than money."

Simon's brow furrowed. "What are you trying to say?"

She shook her head, her appetite gone. "I don't know. Maybe you need to decide if you're going to be a real dad to Opal or not."

"Meaning?"

"She's going to need you around."

His face hardened. "If I hadn't moved here, and hadn't seen you at church that day, I wouldn't know Opal even existed. You had no intention of ever telling me. Having me around wouldn't have been an option then."

Cat clenched her hands into fists. "I didn't tell you because I didn't want you popping in and out of her life like some Santa Claus bearing gifts a couple times a year."

Disappointment shone from his eyes, deep, dark pools of it.

"Cat, I'm doing the best I can here, but I'm not made to stay in one place."

Her mouth went dry as guilt seared her conscience. "Have you ever tried?"

"For the last six months, and it hasn't worked out. I'm going back to what I know."

"But you know jewelry."

"Yes."

Cat took a drink of pop. There wasn't much she could say to that sparse response.

Simon had said that he'd found God in Maple Springs, so why didn't that endear this place to him? He'd even found success with his jewelry shop, but evidently both those things were not enough to make him stay. Neither was finding Opal here or her.

Maybe she'd been mistaken to think they'd had a connection when they'd first met. Maybe what she'd felt with Simon had only been a kindred spirit with a love for adventure. As a photojournalist for a travel magazine, Cat knew that rush well. She missed it too, but things change and responsibilities shift.

Or at least, they did for her.

Cat had come home in spite of fearing her past because it was best for Opal. She'd faced Sue Jensen at the tree lighting and she'd done all right. She hadn't fallen apart. She still worried about being a good mother, but she had no choice but to try her best for Opal. No matter how hard it got at times when her fears took over.

The worst of it was that even though everyone had told her the drowning had been an accident, it wouldn't have mattered had she done it on purpose. The end result would be the same.

Now she feared her future because Simon didn't want to be a part of it. Not more than a sketchy part, anyway. No matter how he provided for Opal or her, the end result was the same. Simon Roberts was not happy here. What if Simon couldn't be happy anywhere and that was what kept him moving?

Cat didn't understand what he was trying to convey, and Simon wasn't sure how to make her see that he wasn't cut out for fatherhood. He'd tried with his sister and brother and failed. Opal would be better off knowing him from a distance as the dad who gave her things but didn't try to mold her into something she wasn't.

Simon brushed his fingertips over Cat's hand. "I'd like something to show that Opal is mine. That I'm her father."

"Why?" It came out as a hoarse whisper.

"I don't carry my father's surname. Roberts was my mother's name."

Cat looked at her plate. "I'm sorry. Opal will know you are her father, I promise."

Simon knew he should have dropped the subject when wariness crept into Cat's eyes, but he kept going. "What about insurance for Opal? I have a good group plan as a small business owner here, but I'll need proof she's mine before I can add Opal as a dependent."

Cat didn't look like she appreciated what he was trying to do. "Opal is covered on mine, so thank you, but no."

Simon narrowed his gaze. He knew about insurance. When he'd made a home for his brother and sister to keep them out of foster care, he'd had to get his siblings on his health plan. He knew how costly it could be to cover a family. Cat had resigned from her job, so either she paid for COBRA coverage to extend the plan her employer had given her—paying for the whole thing out of her own pocket—or she'd applied through the marketplace. He could provide better, without the additional cost to her. "Think about it."

She looked at him. "And then what?"

Simon wanted to pull his hair out at her obstinacy but kept his voice quiet and even. "And then you will have options."

"And so will you."

He sat back down and gathered up her hands between his own. Looking her in the eyes, he hoped to convey his sincerity. "I would never try to take away custody of Opal. She's far better off with you than me."

She squeezed his hands in return, but her eyes clouded over. Whether she doubted him or herself, he wasn't sure.

Looking over the now cool pizza and wings, he spread his hands. "I can rewarm everything."

She took a slice of lukewarm pizza. "This is fine. Thanks for dinner."

"You're welcome." He grabbed a couple of slices and they ate in silence.

Cat hadn't finished half of her slice before Opal fussed and then cried from lying on her belly a few feet away. "Want me to get her?" Simon offered.

"Finish eating, I'll get her." Cat went to her.

Simon leaned his head back and stared at the ceiling. Cat didn't trust him. Was her protectiveness normal? It wasn't as if he could ask someone. Anyone he knew well enough to even broach such a subject was part of Cat's family.

Zach had once said Cat had a rough time of it growing up. What did that mean? Perhaps her father might have some insight. If nothing else, Andy had been a dad ten times over. He had experience that might prove helpful.

Cat returned to the table with a cooing Opal in her arms. Watching them, he was struck by the feeling of how right it felt having them here.

He noticed a darkening spot on the leg of Opal's pants. "Is she wet?"

Cat felt it and nodded. Then she looked around for the diaper bag.

There wasn't a good place to change her diaper at his place other than the floor or his bed. They'd already experienced a roll off the couch, so no sense in repeating that one. Simon had nothing in the way of baby things.

He'd ordered a crib and a changing table, but it'd take time before they were delivered.

Cat gently rocked Opal in her arms as she fetched the diaper bag and knelt on the living room floor.

Opal whined a little.

"It's okay, baby. Let's get you cleaned up and dry." Cat's voice sounded soft.

She was the picture of motherhood, a natural who seemed to know just what to do.

"Is she okay?"

"She's fine, just needs changing."

Simon gathered his courage and approached them. "Will you show me how to do this?"

Cat gave him an odd look. "Why?"

"I don't know." He shrugged. Suddenly, he wanted to prove to her that he could do it. "What if you step away from the store or something and she needs changing while I'm the only one there?"

"So, I can bring her every day?"

"For a while, yes." He didn't quite trust himself working alone with Cat, and perhaps the baby might dampen any ardent ideas he had about kissing her.

Cat looked at him a good long while before she patted the floor next to her. "First thing you need is the changing mat. It's in the diaper bag pocket here."

Simon joined her on the living room floor.

Cat grabbed the square mat and laid it on the floor. She settled Opal on her back, pulled off her fuzzy socks and tickled the baby's feet before pulling off the soft cotton pink pants printed with gray elephants.

Opal kicked. She had his darker skin tone over Cat's creamy complexion.

"Are you going to give me a go?" Simon knelt down beside her.

Cat backed away, but only a little. "All right. Here's a diaper and wipes and a fresh pair of pants."

Simon awkwardly took charge. He took off the wet diaper and folded and rolled it into a neat little square before moving on to the wipes. When he was done with those, he picked up the clean diaper, turning it a couple of times. "Which way does it go?"

Cat gave a quick tutorial. "Just remember, tabs in the back so they fold over in the front."

"Here we go, Princess." He lifted Opal's feet and the baby gurgled and smiled.

Cat shook her head.

"How do you get the tabs to stick?"

"Pull them loose like so." Cat reached over to show him and her shoulder rubbed against his.

He turned his head the same time she did, bringing them nose to nose again. "I think I have it now. Thanks."

Cat searched his eyes.

He stopped breathing, but before he could lean closer, Cat backed away.

"It's late. We'd better go."

He watched as she clicked the top of the wipes tub closed and stuffed it in the diaper bag, along with Opal's discarded pants.

He finished snapping Opal's pink onesie before slipping on soft gray pull-on pants, followed by her socks and fleece booties. A fleece jacket, hat and matching mittens came next.

"Simon?"

He picked up Opal and cuddled her close. "Yes?"

"What time do you want me at the store?"

He looked at her. "Same time. One?"

"Perfect." Cat reached out her hands. "Want me to take her?"

Simon waved her away and stood. "I'll hold her while you gather her things. Take some pizza with you."

Cat thoughtfully tipped her head. "Maybe just a slice or two."

Simon walked around the room with Opal while Cat wrapped up some pizza and donned her coat. When he finally handed over the baby, he said, "Every kid deserves to know who her father is."

"It'll be years before Opal will ask. Will you be around when she does?"

He deserved the question, even though it hit him like a blow to the stomach. He hadn't given Cat any kind of timetable for when he'd return or how often. Perhaps because leaving felt a lot like running away. Simon had always been good at running away.

Chapter Nine

By the end of the week, Cat had fallen into a nice routine with Opal at Simon's jewelry shop. She arrived around one. The baby slept on the way there and for a while more at the shop. Then Cat fed her, and she and Simon played with Opal before the baby slept some more through the customer traffic and noise from Simon in his workshop.

Today he'd knocked that routine off track by telling her she needn't come in until later for the shoppers' walk. Since her parents were also attending the event, Cat decided to take Opal with her to Simon's shop and had packed extra warm clothes for later. She'd also baked cookies and clipped some pine boughs to use in a vase on the counter. First up, get Opal settled inside, and then she'd fetch the rest.

Using a store key, Cat entered through the back, carrying Opal in her car seat, the diaper bag and another bag.

"There you are." Simon smiled. "Whoa, what's all that?"

"Stuff for walking around town." Cat set everything down. "I have more. Can you watch Opal?"

Simon took the car seat. "Definitely."

In minutes, she returned with a Christmas tin filled

with sugar cookies, a vase and pine clippings and a few leftover pinecone sticks.

Simon gave her a quizzing look as he removed Opal's pink fleece hat and carefully lifted her from the car seat. Gently, he cradled her without disturbing her slumber.

Cat slipped out of her mother's puffy down coat and hung it up. She proceeded to fill the heavy cut-glass vase with water and made fresh cuts on the ends of the greenery before arranging it. She slipped in pinecone sticks that she'd coated with shimmering spray-on snow.

Simon stepped close. "What's that for?"

"To bring a little Christmas inside the store." Cat scooted away and set the vase on the counter.

"Looks nice, but it may be wasted if no one comes in. It's been pretty dead in here."

"Give it some time. It's only five thirty."

Simon laid Opal down in her travel crib. "I don't know how to do that thing you do with the blanket."

Cat nodded and swaddled up Opal. The baby jerked awake when Cat slipped on her matching flannel cap, but soon drifted back to sleep. Cat was blessed with a good sleeper—that was for certain.

Cat fetched the tin.

Simon was at her elbow. "And this?"

Cat opened the tin and laughed when his eyes lit up. "Cookies. Have one."

"You made these?" Simon bit into one and closed his eyes. "These are good. Really good."

Cat set the tin near the vase.

"One more." Simon grabbed two.

"What's your favorite?"

He lifted his hand. "So far, these."

"Have you never baked cookies before?"

He shook his head. "No. My sister used to make chocolate chip on occasion."

He rarely referenced his family. With what she knew about his mother's issues, she could understand, but what about his brother and sister? "Do your siblings know where you are? That you moved here?"

His gaze clouded over. "No."

"Why not?"

"I haven't talked to either in years. At my mother's funeral, it was pretty clear my sister didn't want anything to do with me. My brother was in jail, so..." He shrugged.

She saw the pain in his eyes. "I'm sorry."

"Some people aren't meant to be a family."

"It takes work to be a close-knit family, commitment." Cat was grateful for her parents' example.

The door jingled as it opened. They both greeted the small group of people that came in and attacked the cookies before milling around only to soon leave without buying anything.

"That was rude," Simon said.

Cat chuckled. "The shoppers' walk isn't really about shopping so much as getting a look at what the merchants have to offer. And sure, some people meander in mostly for the treats. It's not only a way to highlight the downtown businesses, but to thank people for their patronage."

"Hmm." He didn't look convinced.

"You're sort of tucked out of the way down here." Cat scrunched her nose. "All the fun stuff's happening in the center of town."

"Then let's go there."

Cat glanced at Opal, still sleeping. "Give it a little time. Let's see if anyone else comes in first."

He nodded. "I checked on the crib and changing table

I ordered for Opal. They'll be delivered to the house early next week."

"Your house?"

"Yes. You said you're using an old crib at your parents'. This way, it'll be set up and ready for you and Opal when you move in."

After he left. "Thank you."

He waved her thanks away. "I was thinking tomorrow might be a nice day to drive to Traverse City so you can pick out whatever you might need to make that second bedroom into a proper nursery."

Cat felt her mouth drop open. "Simon—"

He held up his hand to stop her. "I want to do this. Let me purchase what you need."

She bit her lip but finally nodded. She didn't say what she was thinking—that what she needed couldn't be bought and paid for.

After an hour with only two more people coming in and leaving without a single purchase, Simon had had enough.

"Let's shut this down and go find the fun stuff." He grabbed another cookie.

Cat bounced an awake Opal on her knee.

The baby gurgled and squealed when Cat stopped, as if urging her to do it again.

"I'll get us ready."

It didn't take long. By the time he'd turned off the lights and grabbed his coat and scarf, Cat had Opal bundled up and under her coat in that wrap carrier. He set the alarm before leading Cat out the door.

A blast of cold air compared to the warmth of the shop met them when they stepped outside. The night was clear with a scatter of stars overhead. It might be near thirty-two degrees, but the temperature was bound to drop as the night wore on. Was it too cold for a baby? He glanced at Cat. Apparently, she didn't think so.

"Thank you for the vase of pine. It makes the store smell like Christmas."

She smiled. "You're welcome."

"So, Traverse City tomorrow?"

Cat shook her head. "Has anyone ever told you that you're awfully persistent?"

He grinned at her. "Can't be in the gem-hunting business without being so."

"You miss it."

How did he explain that it wasn't so much missing the travel or haggling for gems, as getting away from the mundane routine he'd had here. Although since seeing Cat, he hadn't had a moment's boredom. "What about you? Will you miss jet-setting all over the globe to highlight the next high-end vacation fad?"

"I already do." Her voice sounded wistful. Even sad.

He didn't like the idea of Cat being sad. "You said something about writing a piece on Maple Springs for freelance work. Are you going to try other areas around here for that?"

She shrugged. "Maybe."

"Is your article done?"

"Not yet. I wanted to add some of this to it too."

"Well, then, we'd better take advantage of everything we can tonight."

Cat looked at him, clearly pleased. "Is that a promise, Simon Roberts?"

Was it? "Yes, it is, Catherine Zelinsky."

Cat pointed. "Starting right now. There's a horse-drawn carriage ride with our name on it."

"All right, then."

They hustled toward the line of people waiting. There weren't many people, and with two carriages, the wait shouldn't be too long. Two blocks in the heart of Maple Springs had been closed off to cars and the area was packed with people. He thought about what Cat had said and wondered how many of them had purchased anything this night. Looking around, he spotted only a few people with shopping bags.

A group of carolers in Victorian-period costumes stood in the center of an intersection. A basket for donations to help a local charity was strategically placed in front like a scene from a Dickens novel.

Simon stopped to toss in a five-dollar bill. "How's Opal?"

Cat adjusted the pink cap so he could see the baby's face.

His holiday princess looked back at him and cooed. Smiling.

Compared to scaling mountains, traipsing through rain forests and diamond mines, becoming a parent might be considered the biggest adventure of his life. He'd traveled part of that road before with his younger siblings. Not only did he find it not to his liking, but it had been a source of constant stress and tension. They'd resented his intervention, cursing his attempts to help steer them down a correct path.

Cat had said that a strong family took commitment. He'd been committed to giving his brother and sister something better than what he'd had, but they'd bucked him at every turn.

"Come on." Cat reached for his hand.

He chuckled. "Where to?"

"I see hot chocolate." She pulled him farther down

the street, away from the carriage-ride line. "It'll keep us warm while we wait."

He looked back and nearly bumped into her when she stopped.

"Never mind. Maybe we *should* get in the carriage line."

"Hot chocolate sounds good."

Cat backed up. "You go ahead. I'll save us a spot in line."

Struck by how fast she'd changed her mind, Simon nodded. "Very well, I'll see you in a few minutes."

He approached the table with two people handing out hot chocolate. Stepping up, Simon reached for two cups and saw a face that looked familiar.

"Mini marshmallows?" The woman offered some on a spoon.

"Definitely." He held out both cups of steaming hot chocolate, trying to place where he'd seen her before.

As he walked away, it dawned on him where he'd met the woman. Last week, at the tree lighting, she'd talked to Cat and for some reason that brief contact had knocked Cat off-kilter. Was this woman the reason Cat had changed her tune about getting hot chocolate? He'd wondered why she'd stopped so abruptly.

Scanning the crowd for her, he spotted a red fuzzy hat in the carriage-ride line. Cat chatted with someone, looking perfectly at ease. Perhaps he'd read too much into her reaction.

Cat caught his gaze and waved. Smiling a little too broadly, deflecting yet again.

Zach had mentioned she'd had a rough time of it growing up, so it seemed that Cat had a story to tell. Simon had one too. His had been a rough childhood, fraught with dysfunction. He knew her home life hadn't been the problem. Something else must have happened. What would it take for her to trust him enough to tell? Perhaps if he let down his guard, she would let down hers.

When he caught up to her, he handed her a cup of hot chocolate, hoping to open the topic. He asked a question he already knew the answer to. "Was that the same woman I met at the tree lighting?"

"Who?" Cat took a sip and then a larger drink. The hot chocolate wasn't that hot.

"The lady at the hot-chocolate stand. I can't remember her name."

She looked that way, as if trying to figure out who he meant, and shrugged. "Can't really tell who it is from here."

More deflection, but before he could remark on it, their turn for the carriage ride had come. As people climbed down, the team of large horses shook their heads, making the bells on their reins jingle and ring.

"Just like the song, you know, 'Jingle Bells.'" Cat grinned and took a quick picture.

"I got it." He jumped up and then offered Cat his free hand.

She took it and climbed aboard. Neither of them spilled a drop of their lukewarm hot chocolate.

He sat down and Cat squeezed in next to him so another couple could share their bench seat. Two more couples sat across from them. This wasn't so much a romantic carriage ride as a group wagon ride, but at least they were given a blanket for their laps. At this close proximity, they'd stay nice and warm.

Opal chose that moment to make her presence known with a mewling whimper.

"Sorry, baby." Cat shifted.

Simon shifted too and draped his arm around the back

of the seat. His gloved fingers ran into another's. The guy at the other end of the bench had the same idea. "Sorry."

The guy gave him a nod.

Simon adjusted his hand to rest on Cat's shoulder and, as if on impulse, he pulled her closer, against his ribs.

She looked up, wide-eyed.

"To make more room." He felt like he had to explain.

This close, he caught the scent of her hot chocolate as she took another sip. At the same moment, the carriage jerked forward, splashing the dark liquid across the top of her lip and end of her nose. She managed to lick her upper lip but didn't realize a spot remained on her nose.

He couldn't reach it with his free hand and didn't want to attempt brushing it off with his other hand, holding his own cup of hot chocolate. It wasn't hot, but he didn't want to risk splashing Opal. So he leaned down and rubbed his nose against hers.

She jerked back. "What are you doing?"

He chuckled. "You have hot chocolate on the end of your nose."

She rubbed it with her mittened hand, smearing hot chocolate foam across her cheek.

"You didn't get it all." He leaned in again, brushing her cheek with his lips.

"Wait…" She turned her head and their lips met and held.

He wasn't about to really kiss Cat on this crowded carriage ride, but he didn't want to move away from her either. He looked into her startled eyes and smiled against her soft, hot-chocolate-sweetened lips. "You taste pretty good."

She surprised him by smiling back against his mouth. "You do too."

Opal squealed, and Simon rolled his head back and laughed.

When the couple across from them launched into "Jingle Bells" at a rather loud volume, he had to admit there was nothing humdrum about this evening.

Later that night, as Cat settled Opal in the old Zelinsky crib, Cat's mom knocked softly on the door.

"Come in." Cat had changed into warm flannel pajamas and sat on the bed, ready to review the pictures she'd taken of the shoppers' walk.

"Is she asleep?"

Cat nodded. "Fast and hard. Tonight was a lot of activity."

Her mom joined her on the bed. "I saw you and Simon on the carriage ride. It looked like you were having a ball singing your hearts out."

Cat smiled, remembering the feel of Simon's arm around her, the light pressure of his lips on hers. "It was great."

"You two seem to be getting along well."

"Yeah." Maybe too well. Cat's feelings were a mixed bag of hopeful expectations and looming disappointments when it came to Simon.

"Sue Jensen was there. Did you talk to her?"

Cat glanced at her feet. The red polish on her toes was chipped. It had been ages since she'd given herself a good pedicure. "No."

"Oh, Cat, you shouldn't be afraid of Sue. I think talking with her might help bring some closure."

Cat didn't think so. Why relive the past any more than she had to, which was practically every day as it was. "I've gotten tons of closure. Nothing can change what happened."

Her mom patted her hand. "No, but maybe you'll see that God can change how you look at it."

Cat still believed God might yet punish her somehow—balance the scales by visiting harm on her in exchange for the harm she'd done. Like waiting for a package that never came but she knew was out there somewhere with her name and address on it. That package would eventually find its way to her.

"Have you told Simon about it?"

Cat looked at her mom. "Why would I do that?"

Her mom shrugged. "I just thought that you two were, you know, getting close."

"Not that close. He wants to provide for Opal, but that's about it."

Was it all for Opal, though? Sure, he wanted to provide for her by giving her a job, but his house was an added bonus. At least until May, when he'd decide if he'd permanently cut ties here or not. If he did decide to leave, she could probably take over his lease, since she'd planned on getting a place of her own eventually. She had some time to figure it out.

Not so much time with Simon, though. He'd leave after Christmas and that was twenty-four days away. An uneasy feeling in the pit of Cat's belly grew. If they continued on this path of teasing each other with near-kisses, might things change? Could she change his mind about leaving?

"Mom, who would I call about establishing Simon as Opal's father—you know, legally?" Regardless of whether he stayed or not, she owed him an acknowledgment of paternity for Opal.

"Maybe call the county offices and they'll direct you."

Cat nodded. "I'll do it Monday."

"I'm glad, Cat. Your father will be too. Opal needs that legal tie and you do as well, just in case."

Simon might leave, but she didn't think he'd completely abandon them. His comments about not being cut out for fatherhood echoed through her thoughts. Would he still feel that way when he was back in his usual life, chasing down gems around the world? What if the old saying of "out of sight, out of mind" became a reality?

Cat's mom smoothed her hair back like she used to when Cat was little. "What is it?"

Cat shook off her dark thoughts. "Nothing. I think I'm going to turn in early. Big day tomorrow."

"Oh?"

"Simon and I are going to Traverse City to purchase things to make his second bedroom into a nursery for Opal."

"What about church?"

"We need to leave early enough to make the stores, so we're not going."

Her mom frowned at that and then grinned. "Would you like me to watch the baby?"

"She's still not taking the bottle real well."

Her mom waved that away. "We'll be fine. You two go have fun."

Cat chuckled. "It's not a date, Mom."

But her mother was already at the door, ready to turn off the light. "It can be, if you make it so."

Cat drew back the covers of her bed. Maybe her mom was onto something there. Instead of trying to keep her feelings for Simon in check, maybe she should give in and see what happens.

Chapter Ten

Simon pulled into his drive next to Cat's car. They'd taken his Jeep in case of snow on the way down and back from Traverse City, but the roads had remained clear with sunny blue skies.

Shutting off the engine, he turned to Cat. "Do you want to come in?"

Cat had been texting her mom to see how Opal fared while she was gone. She looked at him with disappointment. "I'd better go. Opal's been a little fussy today."

Simon nodded. "No problem."

"Can I come tomorrow? You know, and arrange everything?"

"Till tomorrow, then."

Cat settled her hand on his arm. "Thank you for all this."

His pulse did an odd dance at the expression of gratitude shining in her eyes. "You're welcome."

She scooted out of his car and into hers, waving before she backed out.

Simon waved back, and then he started the task of unloading the packages. He'd had a good time today. Shopping for Opal with Cat was something he'd never pictured himself enjoying. Not in a million years, but there was something very sweet about the way Cat picked things out for their daughter. He could easily envision Opal using the newly purchased rattles and toys. He could see her surrounded by all the pretty blankets too. It didn't take long for him to get caught up in choosing items, as well.

As he entered his rented house with a handful of bags, the quiet emptiness hit him once again, screaming out that this was no way to live. His return to gem hunting beckoned like never before. It wasn't so much the thrill of the hunt, but the comfort he took in knowing the trade so well. He fit into that life in a way he couldn't imagine fitting here.

Dropping the bags on the floor, he pulled out his phone and called the woodworker who was making Opal's crib and changing table. "Hello, this is Simon Roberts. Sorry to call on a Sunday, but I wondered if there was a possibility of having that crib and table delivered sometime tomorrow."

Simon smiled when the fellow informed him that he was finishing it up today and that delivery on Monday would work. After disconnecting, he swiped his contacts and stopped at his sister's phone number. The last time he'd spoken to her had been when she called him because of their mother's sudden death. That had been nearly four years ago.

What kind of reception would he receive if he called her now, out of the blue? They'd lost touch over the years until Margo had tracked him down to tell him about their mother's funeral arrangements. She'd been frosty toward him then, even when he'd offered to pay for the funeral in its entirety. Margo hadn't wanted his money, but he'd paid for it anyway.

Thinking over Cat's words about how providing for a

child takes more than money, Simon's gut twisted. Money was the only sure thing he had to offer the people he considered his family. It was all he'd ever had as an adult. For five years, he'd tried to make a home for his siblings, but it hadn't ended well. Not for any of them. He'd failed then. He couldn't give his sister and brother what they'd needed all those years ago, so why would he be any different for Opal?

The next day, Cat pulled into Simon's driveway around noon. She looked forward to making that second bedroom into a nursery for Opal and she wouldn't mind more time spent with Simon.

Before she even knocked, he opened the door. "Hello."

"Hello. Could you take Opal? I have a few things to bring in." Cat handed over the baby in her car seat.

Simon peeked under the fleece blanket. "Hello, Princess."

Hearing her daddy's voice, Opal cooed.

Cat watched as he went inside, telling Opal all about the special room they were making for her. She briefly closed her eyes before pulling out the Crock-Pot of vegetable beef soup she'd made. She didn't want Simon to leave, but if he did, she'd give him every reason she could to miss her and Opal.

When she entered the house, Simon had Opal out of her car seat and settled into the baby swing.

He looked up. "What do you have there?"

"Vegetable beef soup for lunch."

Simon smiled. "Did you make it?"

Cat set the Crock-Pot on the counter and plugged it in. "I did."

He came near her, very near. He smelled good; the

slight spiciness of his cologne was unique to him. "Good news. The crib is coming today."

Cat blew at a lock of hair that fell across her cheek. "That was fast."

"About a week or so." He reached for her loose hair and anchored it behind her ear. "Thank you for the soup."

"You're welcome." She smiled, hoping to quiet the flutters in her belly that his touch roused. Focus. She owed him more than a pot of soup and some bread, but she'd get into that later.

This morning she'd called the county where Opal had been born. They'd directed her to the right department, which instructed her to download the affidavit of parentage form. She'd printed off a couple of copies, which were tucked inside the diaper bag.

"Is it ready?" Simon rested his hand on her shoulder.

Tempted to lean into him, Cat pulled away when she heard Opal utter a cranky-sounding whine. "It is. I'll slice up some bread too."

Cat checked on the baby. The swing had stopped, so she wound it up to a gentle rocking speed. In moments, Opal settled, staring glassy-eyed at the flames dancing in the fireplace. She'd fall asleep soon.

Simon pulled bowls from the cupboard and then two glasses. "Water or soda?"

"Water is fine." Cat pulled a loaf of bread from a brown paper bag.

"Did you make that too?" Simon's eyes were wide with wonder.

"My culinary skills go only so far. I bought this at the bakery in town." She grabbed the cutting board near the sink, nearly bumping into Simon.

He cupped her elbow.

Cat looked into his soft brown eyes. "Why don't you sit down and I'll get it?"

Simon did so but watched her every move.

Cat ignored the hike in her pulse and ladled steaming soup into a bowl and placed that in front of him, along with the cutting board with the sliced bread. Butter and salt and pepper were already on the table, so she dished up a bowl for herself before sitting down. "It might need more salt."

He gave her a lopsided smile as he tasted it. "It's good."

"I'm glad." She searched his eyes, ready to spill the big news. The news he'd be pleased to hear. "Simon, I downloaded a form that will legally name you as Opal's father."

He paused midway in raising his spoon and his expression froze.

Cat gripped the edge of the table. "Have you changed your mind?"

His eyes cleared. "Not at all."

"Then what is it? Why the hesitation?"

He shrugged, returning to eating.

Cat stared at her bowl of soup at a loss. She thought he'd be happy, satisfied at the very least, but she'd been wrong. "You don't reveal much about yourself, do you?"

He looked surprised by her question. "What do you want to know?"

"You want to be Opal's father, yet you don't. How come?"

His expression hardened. "It's not Opal."

"Then what is it?"

He let out a soft sigh. "I didn't grow up like you. The only time I've done anything remotely close to being a father ended badly. I was twenty-one and living in London when I got a call from my mother the night she'd been arrested. She begged me to save my brother and sister from the foster-care system."

Cat remained quiet, yet afraid of that troubled look in his eyes.

He continued, "For five years, I worked as a jeweler at my employer's store in New York. No traveling—I stayed put so I could look after them. I made sure Margo and Barry had everything they needed, a nicer place to live with better schools, and yet…" Simon looked away, defeated.

She reached for his hand. "What? What happened?"

His expression hardened. "They hated me for it. Hated that I was strict, hated that I made them go to school."

"How old were they when you came back?"

"Fourteen and twelve."

Cat could only imagine the turmoil he'd been through with two teenagers.

"I did my best, but Margo dropped out of college to elope. The marriage didn't last. Barry refused to finish high school after I caught him cutting class. He moved out when he was seventeen, taking several of my valuables with him." Pain streaked through his dark eyes.

Seventeen—the same age Simon had been when his mother had kicked him out. "You can't blame yourself for their decisions."

"Who else is there?" he snorted.

"Well, your mother had a lot to do with it," Cat pointed out.

"Of course there's that, but I can't shift all the blame on her. I had five years with them. I made sure they had a hot meal every night, clean clothes and an allowance. I thought giving them a glimpse at something better would be enough to motivate them to succeed. It had been for me, but it wasn't for them. They resented me for it. They stole from me and lied like my mother used to. Even my employer lied to me."

"Your boss?" What did that have to do with anything?

"I can't prove it, but I believe the thugs who'd chased us all over the highlands were hired by him."

"Why?"

Simon shrugged. "Maybe he was tired of my cut. A few years ago, I started taking payment in first choice of gemstones. That supply helped me start this shop, actually."

A knock at the door was an unwelcome interruption. She was finally getting somewhere, learning something about him that explained so much.

Simon got up. "That's the furniture. Opal's awake now."

Cat turned. Sure enough, Opal lay wide-eyed in the swing, reaching for the fuzzy animals overhead, only to miss and try again. Cat reached over and checked Opal's diaper. Still dry. For now.

Cat rehashed the wounded intensity in Simon's voice. He'd been deeply hurt by the betrayal of the ones closest to him. Family and his boss. She'd iced the cake of deception by not telling him he had a daughter.

The sound of the door slamming against the wall startled her. She glanced at the baby.

Opal scrunched up her face, ready to wail.

Cat reached for her and cuddled her close. "It's okay, Opal. Hush now, baby."

Simon and another man carried a huge rectangular object covered in a moving blanket through the door, bumping the wall as they went.

Cat angled the swing out of the draft of the opened door and stepped closer to the crackling fire. She returned Opal to the swing, turning up the gentle motion to rock a little faster, and then followed the men down the hall, looking forward to a peek at this handcrafted crib.

She entered the bedroom as they were coming out, getting in the way. "Sorry."

Simon wrapped his arm around her waist, steering her back where she'd come from. "Stay with Opal while we bring in the table. I want you to wait to see them together, all set up."

"Okay." The warmth of his touch shattered any argument she might have offered. Hearing Opal fuss once again, she rushed to pick her up. "Oh, sweetie, I'm sorry."

She bundled the fleece blanket around Opal and snuggled her close, chasing away a chill that raced in from the opened door. She stepped closer to the fire and watched Simon and the other man bring in the next piece.

The table was narrower and easier to maneuver than the crib, so it didn't take long to bring in. In minutes, the work was done and Simon walked the delivery guy out and thanked him with a tip.

Once the door was again closed, Cat whispered, "Hurry. I want to see the furniture."

Simon reached for her hand. "Come on, then."

She gladly took it and gave him a reassuring squeeze. Simon had fears too. Different perhaps than hers, but just as real. Did he fear that Opal might walk away and reject him like his family had? Like the company he'd worked for since he'd been seventeen?

Hanging on tight to Simon's hand, Cat stopped at the closed door of the second bedroom.

He looked at her. "Ready?"

"Uh, yeah." Cat felt like a kid awaiting a Christmas gift.

Simon opened it and stepped back, letting her enter first.

Cat couldn't speak because of the sudden swell of emotion that closed up her throat and blurred her vision with tears.

"The sides come off so it can be converted into a twin bed. You know, when Opal is older. Do you like it?" Simon sounded worried.

She loved it. The crib was made of a mellow oak in a sleigh shape. The changing table was the same wood and echoed that same style. She'd never seen anything so exquisite. The pair must have cost a fortune. "Simon—"

He wrapped his arm around her shoulders. "It's okay if you don't."

"Oh, no. I love it. It's beautiful. It's just…" Cat sniffed and gripped Opal tighter, thinking about when their daughter was older and using a twin bed. Would she have two parents supporting her or just one?

Like so many things since having Opal, Cat had no control over what happened next. Would Simon ever want to be a real family? Too soon to tell. She owed him the truth about her past too, so that he'd understand her own fears. But would telling him what happened the summer she'd turned sixteen draw him closer or push him further away?

"Looks like we're done." Simon stepped back and surveyed the bright orange curtains with a tribal white dot-and-slash pattern. He turned to Opal, who was rocking in her baby swing. "Nice, huh? How do you like your room?"

Opal looked around as if she'd understood his words. Simon laughed. "This looks really great."

"It does." Cat had picked out matching crib sheets in a bright, cheerful watercolor-styled print of orange lions with bright yellow manes painted like flower petals on a white background.

A quilt with blocks of both prints lay folded over the oak rocking chair they'd picked up at a specialty baby store.

They took in the nursery. His rental agreement didn't allow for painting, so they'd purchased wall decals that stuck rather well. A lion, a giraffe and some tall grasses. Lovely.

He turned toward Cat. She was lovely too. More so each day. Or perhaps more so today because she seemed to understand his failure with his family.

Opal uttered a weak cry. Not her usual ear-splitting holler, but Cat picked her up and Opal nuzzled against her.

"I'd better feed her." Cat's face flushed when she caught him watching them.

Simon nodded and made his way to the door. "Give the new room a go. Try out the crib too."

He walked through his rental house, filled with the aroma of homemade soup that mixed well with the warmth of the fireplace. Snow fell outside and it dawned on him that this place didn't feel empty now. This was the closest he'd ever been to feeling like he had a real home and a normal family. Only it wasn't normal. They weren't married and they'd made no commitment other than Cat agreeing to legally name him as Opal's father.

He still wanted to leave come the first of the year, travel to Africa for tourmaline and rubies in Mozambique, but at the same time he wanted to come back. He wanted to return to Cat and Opal if they'd have him.

Simon dropped onto the couch and ran his hands through his hair, staring into the flames. Could they make this work?

"Simon?"

He looked into Cat's concerned eyes. How long had he been sitting there? "Yes?"

"Come see Opal."

He got up and followed Cat down the short hall. She pushed open the door for him, so he entered the room. *The nursery.* The curtains had been drawn to dim the late-afternoon light.

Peeking into the crib, he saw that Opal lay wrapped in a blanket. His little princess had her eyes closed. Her silky hair stuck out from under her sleep cap, giving her a cherubic quality. His heart twisted painfully in his chest.

This was *his daughter.*

"She loves the crib."

Simon nodded, but the room seemed to be closing in on him. He needed some space. Some air. "I'm going to run to the store and grab dinner. Anything you might like?"

Cat blinked her eyes. "Uh, I hadn't planned on staying, but now that Opal's sleeping, I guess we're not going anywhere. Whatever you get is fine."

Simon touched her arm, knowing that it'd be worse returning to an empty house after seeing his daughter snuggled into her own crib. "Stay. I won't be long."

"Okay."

Simon slipped into his coat and exited the door. The blast of cold air did little to unravel the hot ball of twining turmoil in his gut. After all those years, the pain of his family's rejection still stung.

His mother had betrayed him countless times, but kicking him out had been the last straw, so he'd left without looking back. Until his mother had been arrested and he'd tried to do right by his sister and brother, but it had been too late. The damage had been done. He'd been out of their lives for several years and had lost all credibility with them. He'd abandoned them after all, something they'd never forgotten or forgiven.

Opal might only be a baby, but would leaving her wreak similar havoc?

He climbed into his Jeep and headed to the local grocery store. Each street he turned onto had holiday lights glowing from inside homes, on porches and trees. Christmas trees placed in front windows gleamed with sparkling light. This was what normal people did. They put up Christmas trees that looked nice. Not the fake snow-coated little tree his mother used to stick on the table, when she bothered to notice it was Christmas.

The snow picked up and huge flakes drifted from the sky to swirl and stick to his windshield. Pulling into the grocery store parking lot, he had no idea what he wanted for dinner. Coming here had only been an excuse.

A section of the lot had been squared off with strings of big white bulbs. The Maple Springs Chapter of Boy Scouts were selling Christmas trees. As if invisible strings drew him, Simon walked toward them. This year he wanted Christmas to be real and something special.

Chapter Eleven

Cat sat in the new rocking chair in the nursery and watched Opal sleep. What had made Simon jump like a scared jackrabbit? So scared that he'd bolted for the door. She didn't buy the dinner excuse. There was plenty of vegetable beef soup left, unless he hadn't cared for it as much as he'd let on.

Cat heard the door open.

Simon.

She heard a scratching noise against the wall as if he were moving something large. Now what was he doing? After checking on Opal, still sleeping, Cat exited the room. "Simon?"

Her heart skipped a beat at the sight of him wrestling with a large Christmas tree. He managed to slide it into an equally large tree stand, but the whole thing leaned to the left. She might as well be butter in a pan, because she'd just melted.

"A little early for a tree." It wasn't, but Cat didn't know what else to say.

Simon gave her a lopsided grin. "Seemed like the thing to do."

Cat let loose something that sounded like a giggle. She

hadn't giggled since… It had been a long time. Once she collected herself, she hurried to help. Crouching down at the base of the tree, she looked over the stand. "I don't think the trunk is in all the way."

"This isn't exactly my forte. In fact, I've never purchased a Christmas tree before this one."

A sad thing to admit. Cat loosened the screws and then looked up. "Go ahead and push it down if you can."

He did so with a resounding grunt. "There."

She turned the screws until they tightened into the bark. "Do you recall if they made a fresh cut?"

"They did, yes."

Looking at the lush Christmas tree, Cat sighed. "Oh, Simon, it's beautiful. Where did you get it?"

"Grocery store parking lot."

The fresh smell of balsam filled the room and the needles were soft to her touch. She wished he'd taken her with him to pick it out, but then that was something couples did. Real families too. They were neither.

Reminded of his comment about the mess of a Christmas tree, Cat blurted out, "What made you buy one?"

He stared at her, as if mulling over the question and searching for a reason. "I thought you might like one."

Her eyes suddenly watered, making her blink. He'd done so much with the nursery and now this.

Simon gave her a soft smile. "Now, don't go crying on me."

Feeling silly, she rolled her eyes and laughed. "I'm not. It's just—"

"Just what?" His voice couldn't sound silkier.

She shook her head. She didn't deserve all this, not after keeping Opal secret from him.

His gaze intensified. "Meeting you did something to me. I never forgot you, and now with Opal—"

"What?" Her voice was barely above a whisper.

"I don't know what." He looked as if he shook it off, then gestured toward the tree. "Where should we put that?"

Cat wasn't going to push him into admitting that they might have something special between them. He had to decide for himself if they had something worth working for—worth coming back for. "Maybe in the corner farthest from the fireplace."

"Good place." He hefted the tree again and set it down.

Cat breathed in fresh pine. "That's perfect. I'll get some water and then tomorrow I'll pick up some lights and decorations—"

He held up his hands, sheathed in leather gloves. "Hang on, I bought some, along with dinner. The bags are in the car."

This was what having her own family would be like. Cat had never wanted a family of her own before. Never thought she'd have a husband, because with one came kids and kids had never been a possibility for her while she lived with such a horrible mistake. Knowing the grief that came with terrible loss had been a strong deterrent to deep relationships, but right now she wanted one. She wanted it all, with Simon.

She watched him leave, her thoughts awhirl.

He'd experienced his share of pain. Loss. He might understand her. He certainly knew what she liked. He'd bought her a Christmas tree! A real one that would make a mess dropping needles on the floor. This was something. Something big.

Tamping down the flutters that stirred inside her, she fetched a pitcher from the cupboard in the kitchen and filled it with lukewarm water.

She heard Simon stamp the snow off his feet in the

other room. He entered the kitchen with a few grocery bags that he placed on the table. "The snow is coming down pretty heavily."

Cat peeked out the kitchen window and saw nothing but a blur of white. "That doesn't look good."

"Visibility was horrible even through town. You should call your mom and let her know you're staying here."

Cat's belly flipped. Staying seemed like a bad idea, but she didn't like the idea of driving with Opal in this weather. "It might clear up."

"We'll see." From one grocery bag, he pulled out two thick submarine-styled sandwiches. "To go with the soup."

So he did like it.

For now, she wasn't going anywhere and neither was he. "I'll get the bowls."

Simon brought his soup bowl to the sink while Cat loaded the dishwasher. The tree had been a good move, bringing them closer together. She filled his house with something he'd never had before and it wasn't simply the aroma of homemade soup. This was something he hadn't known *could* exist. This felt terribly close to contentment.

He heard Opal fuss from the other room, a cranky sound.

Cat leaned for the dish towel and wiped her hands.

"I'll get her."

"Thanks."

Simon headed for the nursery. Stepping into the spare bedroom, he took it all in. From the cheerful lion-print linens to a long-necked giraffe decal on the wall. All reminiscent of Africa. Not the highlands where they'd met, but the plains and grasslands in Kenya that had been the main subject of the article she'd written. The only one he'd ever read of hers.

"Hello, Princess."

She mewed, her face flushed red from crying.

He unwrapped Opal from her swaddling blanket and picked her up. Her diaper crunched together as if she might be wet, so he changed her like Cat had showed him.

Using the new changing table made things easy with everything within reach. After tapping Opal's nose and tickling her belly, Simon snapped her long cotton bottoms closed and then picked her up. He also grabbed a thick quilt they could spread on the floor in the living room.

The baby kicked her legs when she spotted Cat.

Cat was checking out the bag of Christmas ornaments he'd purchased. "Hi, Opal, do you want to play on the floor?"

Simon loved the sound his daughter made when she cooed, but then she squealed when he handed her over to Cat.

"I changed her." He spread the quilt on the floor.

"Great, thanks." After laying Opal on her belly, Cat returned to the bag of boxed ornaments. "Let's see what you bought for the tree."

He stretched out on the floor near the baby. He hadn't known what Cat might like, so he'd picked out basic red glittery balls and white lights. A bunch of small red velvet bows, since she seemed to like those when they'd hung garland at his shop. "Simple stuff."

She smiled at him. "Perfect stuff. Do you have plain popcorn?"

He nodded, feeling like he'd slayed some dragon for her and had returned with its treasure. "I think I still have a bag in the cupboard. Why?"

"We can string popcorn for the tree." He heard the

sound of cupboard doors being opened and closed. "Found it."

"We?"

She peeked her head around the corner from the kitchen, bag of popcorn in hand. "You and me."

"I'm starting to like the sound of you and me." It had been two weeks since first seeing Cat at church. His life had been turned upside down and then oddly righted.

Tonight felt incredibly right.

She smiled back, surprised. "Me too."

He tickled under Opal's chin. The baby lifted her head a little, wobbled and rolled to her side. Simon righted her and she kicked her legs as if swimming. "She's changed in these last couple of weeks. She's more aware or something."

"She's growing fast."

Opal started to fuss, uttering a sharp cry of discontent.

"Come on now, Princess." Simon picked her up and headed for the rocker, pulling it closer to the fireplace.

The baby quieted as he rocked back and forth, watching Cat open the strings of lights.

Cat tipped her head, thinking about something.

He stared back. "What is it?"

"I was just wondering. Maybe you should let your sister or brother know you're here, living in Northern Michigan."

It hadn't even occurred to him to let them know that he was living stateside again. Another failure. "I can't imagine it making a bit of difference to them."

"What's your sister's name?" Cat plugged in a set of lights and they shimmered a soft golden white.

"Margo."

Cat reached for Opal. The baby had stuck her whole fist in her mouth. "And your brother?"

"Barry."

Lifting the baby from his arms, Cat whispered, "It's Christmas, Simon. Maybe you should reach out to them and see what happens."

That very thing had been heavy on his mind lately. Especially after finding God. It seemed as though the Lord would want him to seek them out, but he'd held back.

He searched Cat's face and lingered on her eyes. They'd spent a lot of time together these past two weeks, but did they know enough about each other? "Perhaps."

She squeezed his shoulder. "I'll feed her and be right back."

Simon watched Cat walk away. Opal was their connection, but would she be enough to keep them together?

Cat fed the baby in the nursery while Simon popped popcorn. She could hear the corn popping and so could Opal. The baby kept turning her head toward the noise, distracted from eating, as if she didn't really want to nurse.

"You okay, baby?" Cat caressed her cheek. "Getting used to a new place?"

Cat was in the same boat as her daughter, looking at things with new eyes. New feelings too. The past couple of days with Simon had been so good, maybe too good. She needed to bring up two subjects she'd rather not talk about—his plans to leave and her past.

Opal squirmed and Cat knew she was done. "Come on, let's go decorate the tree."

Walking toward the living room, she heard Christmas music.

Simon threw another log on the fire and looked up as she entered.

"Nice touch." Cat nodded toward the stylish radio where the soft instrumental song of "Jingle Bells" played.

"I thought so."

"You thought right." Cat settled Opal in the swing.

A large bowl of plain popcorn had been placed on the coffee table, waiting to be strung. Suddenly antsy to see the tree decorated, she didn't care to take the time to string that popcorn now. "Why don't we add the popcorn later? It takes a while to make garland."

"We've got plenty of time and nowhere to go." Simon looked outside. "Did you call your mom?"

"Yes. She said the roads were bad."

"Then stay. I'll sleep on the couch."

Cat chewed her lip but nodded. This might be interesting.

"I need to grab some more wood. Be back in a minute." Simon caressed Opal's cheek on the way out, as he always did.

Cat emptied the rest of the grocery bag. He'd purchased three boxes of one-hundred-count lights. Glancing at the fat tree, Cat thought it'd be sparse coverage. Simon would never be accused of excess. He was a measured man. Guarded. Rarely putting anything on display, physically or emotionally. He kept his past locked up nearly as tight as hers, rarely talking about it.

After connecting each set of lights, Cat plugged them in and started swirling them into the top branches of the tree with the help of one of the dining room chairs. The first strand was nearly done by the time Simon entered with a canvas bag full of logs.

"It looks nice already."

"I think so." Cat got down from the chair and wove the second strand around the tree.

He stood next to her. "I should have purchased another string of lights."

More like three, but she wasn't saying it. Back up on

the chair, Cat rearranged the lights to cover more. "I can make these work."

Simon helped her space them out.

She reached for one of the back branches and the chair wobbled.

"Easy." Simon grabbed her waist. "Here, let me do that."

"I've got it." She looped the lights a little lower. "There."

As she prepared to climb down, Cat's breath caught when Simon scooped her up in his arms. She gripped his shoulders. "Warn me when you're going to do that."

He loosened his hold enough for her to slide down until her feet touched the floor, but he didn't let go. His hands rested on her hips as he searched her eyes. "Kiss me, Catherine."

Cat glanced at his mouth for a split second. "We shouldn't."

"Yes, we should." He lowered his lips to hers, gently at first and then with more pressure until she responded.

Wrapping her arms around Simon's neck, Cat returned his kiss with enthusiasm. It felt like she'd finally come home to a place where she wanted to stay. For good.

Pulling back, she needed to tell him everything, find out how he'd take it and go from there. Cat braced her hands against Simon's chest. "Simon, listen, I need to tell you—"

"Later, Cat. Talk later." He kissed her again.

Only to be interrupted when Opal let out an ear-splitting cry.

Simon woke up to the thundering sound of a plow truck scraping the road out in front of his house. He sat up quickly and rubbed his eyes.

Cat—

She'd slept in Opal's room on cushions pulled from the couch and extra blankets. The baby had fussed quite a bit while they'd decorated the tree and throughout the night. He'd heard her cry a few times in the wee hours too, but it was quiet now. Very quiet.

He checked the time on the clock near his bed. Eight o'clock. He got up and threw on a sweatshirt. Stopping outside the door to Opal's room, he listened. All quiet in there. Had they left? He padded toward the kitchen and spotted Cat's purse on the table. No. They were still here.

He noticed that his phone flashed with a new text message. Swiping the screen, he saw that it came from Cat's father, almost an hour ago. Opening the message, Simon read an invitation to breakfast at the diner in town.

Simon took a deep breath and texted back that he could be there in an hour, after he shoveled his driveway. A quick response of agreement from Andy gave Simon the impression that there was something weighing on the man's mind. Simon had a few questions of his own, especially after last night.

Kissing Cat, he realized he had found someone worth coming back for. Even with Opal's fussing, which had put a damper on the evening, Simon wanted to provide more than simply financial support for them both. Could he build a life here in Maple Springs? It'd be good for Opal. Good for Cat too, but could he open up enough to adjust?

Simon wanted details of how Andy Zelinsky had been a good father with a big family when he'd been stationed all over during his military career. How had he done it?

It didn't take long before Simon was showered and dressed. He left a note on the table near Cat's purse, letting her know that he'd take over the jewelry shop today and she needn't come in. After she'd been up with Opal most of the night, he wanted her to stay home and rest.

Stepping outside, he was shocked at the amount of snow that had fallen. He waded through the fluffy white stuff that reached halfway up his shins and reached for a shovel in the garage. He doubted it was any better at the Zelinsky house, and yet Andy had wanted to drive ten miles into town for breakfast?

Simon's gut twisted. This must be really important.

He made quick work of shoveling his short driveway and made his way into town, parked his car and walked into the diner owned by Cat's brother and his wife. The incredible aroma of fresh bacon and coffee stirred his empty stomach, making it rumble.

"Hey, Simon," Cam called out from the grill area.

"Good morning. Mind if I sit at a table near the window?"

"Go ahead. I'll let Rose know. Coffee?"

"Hot tea, actually."

Cam gave him a nod. "Got it."

Simon slipped into one of two red vinyl-covered chairs that matched a retro-style square table with silver legs. There were only a few patrons seated at the stools along the counter. Perhaps the weather had kept more customers away.

Simon stared out the large window overlooking Main Street, watching for Cat's father. Other merchants shoveled the walkways in front of their respective shops while a small tractor plow cleared the sidewalks. The heavy snowfall from the night before had changed to light snowflakes falling haphazardly from a pale gray sky.

Seeing the tall man enter the Hometown Grille, Simon stood. He might be a man over forty, but he felt every bit an awkward youth around Cat's father.

He extended his hand. "Mr. Zelinsky, good morning."

"Call me Andy." Cat's father gave him a vigorous handshake in return. "I understand Cat stayed at your house last night."

"Because of the weather." Simon felt compelled to explain.

Andy nodded. "Michigan winters can be tough. How are you holding up?"

Surprised by that concern-laced question, Simon responded with candor. "Pretty fair. Although I may need to invest in a snowblower."

If he truly planned to stay.

Cat's father chuckled. "They come in handy."

Simon got down to business, spearheading what this meeting might be about. "I'd also like to be a proper dad, but I don't really know how."

Rose arrived with a small pot of hot water and a cup, along with a box of various tea bags. She also brought along a mug of black coffee for Andy. She set a dish of creamers down, as well. "We're serving a sweet or savory waffle special today. Your choice of two pumpkin waffles with pecans, bacon and maple syrup or corn bread waffles with sausage gravy and two fried eggs."

Simon thanked her, as did Andy, when she handed them two menus. "I'll be back in a few minutes."

"Look, Simon, there's no easy answer to that. Commitment is a big part. How committed are you to the baby and Cat if you're leaving?"

That was a direct hit, so Simon hit back. "I understand you were stationed away from Maple Springs for long stretches during your military career."

Andy tipped his head. "True."

"Gem hunting is something I do not want to give up."

Simon dunked his tea bag until the water turned dark and strong.

"Ready to order?" Rose smiled.

Simon hadn't even looked at the menu, so he decided on the sweet waffle special. Andy ordered the same, along with a refill on his coffee. He'd guzzled his first cup.

"Any advice on being a father would be greatly appreciated."

Andy looked thoughtful. He was a stern-looking man to boot. "Be flexible, but expect the best from them and they'll deliver."

Sage words, but not anything like what he'd experienced with Margo and Barry. He'd expected far more than they had delivered. He needed practical advice, not slogans. Simon sipped his tea.

"Above all else, love them and pray daily."

Simon nodded, even though he knew love wasn't always enough. Every person he'd ever trusted had crushed his love with rejection or lies.

Cat had, in a sense, lied to him by never telling him about Opal, but the lie was at least somewhat understandable. She'd been protective of Opal and perhaps rightly so. They hadn't known much about each other.

There was still so much he wanted to learn about her. Last night, Cat had wanted to talk about something, but they'd been sidetracked by Opal, who'd fussed all night. Zach's words that Cat hadn't had an easy time of it growing up echoed through his thoughts.

Looking at Cat's father, he asked straight out, "Is there something that happened to Cat? Something I should know?"

Andy rubbed his chin and leaned back but didn't answer right away. "All that is in the past. It's Cat's story to tell, not mine."

That didn't ease his mind at all; if anything, it only made matters worse. It was obvious that something *had* happened, but Andy wasn't sharing his daughter's tale. Terrible things crossed Simon's mind only to be discarded. Cat's family was genuine and loving, so he didn't think the problem lay there. Cat hadn't feared him in Africa, so it couldn't be about men, in general or specific.

She'd been enthralled with the Welo opal adventure, even though they'd been chased. She'd been afraid but had thanked him for a great time after he'd put her on that plane back to Addis Ababa.

Andy set his mug of coffee down with a thud. "Cat cares for you. I can tell. What her mother and I want to know is, what are you prepared to do about it?"

"Do?" The warmth of hearing Cat cared paled in light of what Andy didn't say. His comment about commitment had been about their expectations. Cat's parents wanted them to tie that knot a little tighter by making his commitment legally binding.

He couldn't really blame him. If the roles were reversed and Opal had been the one in Cat's shoes, Simon would probably expect the same.

Andy merely raised his eyebrow.

"Give us some time." Simon was just getting used to the idea of a lifetime commitment.

Again, Andy nodded, appearing satisfied with that answer.

Opal tied him and Cat together, sure, but Simon wanted their knot to be secure. It wasn't. Not yet. Not after only a few kisses.

Chapter Twelve

Cat stared at their Christmas tree and yawned. She'd finished decorating it while Opal slept. The baby wouldn't nurse much. After a short and fussy feeding that morning, she'd fallen asleep while Cat rocked her, so she'd tucked Opal in the crib and taken a quick shower. Too bad she had to put back on the clothes she'd worn the day before, but she'd head home and change into something fresh after Opal's nap.

Bright sunlight shone in through the windows, making the glittery red Christmas balls glimmer and shine. Maybe she'd buy some extra lights. Or maybe not. He'd even strung popcorn while Opal had fussed through their evening together. Simon had given her this tree as a gift, so she didn't want to change a thing.

Simon.

Her heart tumbled every time she thought about him. The kisses they'd shared had been tentative, even sort of searching, as if testing this new dynamic out—until they'd been interrupted by Opal.

Staying over had been awkward too. Simon had tried to insist on her taking his room, but Cat had put her foot down about sleeping near Opal in case she woke up.

She had, with a vengeance. Cat hoped Simon had slept through it all, but she didn't know. Simon had left early this morning, while she and Opal had finally grabbed some sleep.

She glanced at the clock. Opal's midday nap was running long. But then, she'd fussed so much overnight that she must be tired. Even though she'd slept late, Cat was tired, as well.

Hearing no sounds from the baby monitor, Cat went in to check on Opal. Entering the nursery, Cat saw that Opal lay still, swaddled as she always was for crib sleep, but something didn't *feel* right.

Cat rushed to the crib and sighed with relief when she saw the even up and down of Opal's breathing. Then she touched her baby's cheek and nearly cried out from how hot her daughter's skin was. She quickly unwrapped the swaddling blanket.

"Opal, Princess, wake up." Cat tickled the baby's sock-covered feet.

Opal's eyes seemed unusually heavy, and when she finally opened them, she didn't focus. Suddenly, she twitched all over. Her toes pointed and her fingers fluttered in a jerky rhythm.

"Oh no, no." Cat turned Opal onto her side and stroked her forehead and back, but the spasms didn't stop. "Stay with me, Princess."

Images from the past clouded her thoughts, but Cat pushed back against the memories of little Muriel Jensen, limp and lifeless on that dock. This wasn't the same!

"God, please don't do this." Tears blurred Cat's eyes, so she wiped them with the heel of her palm.

Opal went limp and Cat froze.

"No!"

Opal uttered a mewling cry.

Cat picked her up and held her close as she searched the changing table for the thermometer she'd used last night. Last night, Opal's temp had been only a little higher than normal. Where was it? Too much time. She grabbed her phone instead and hit her mother's name.

"Come on, come on. Mom!"

"Cat, what is it? What's wrong?"

"Opal must be sick. She's burning up and I think she just had a seizure—"

"You're still at Simon's?"

"Yes."

"I'm in town. I'll be right there."

"Hurry!" Cat pocketed her phone and resumed her search for the thermometer. Finding the thermometer by the bathroom sink, where she'd left it after washing it, Cat stashed it in the diaper bag and ran into the living room. She didn't dare lay Opal down for fear that something might happen and Cat wouldn't see or hear her.

Why was her baby so quiet? Last night she'd hollered enough to bring the house down, but now— Cat slammed her feet into her boots. Why hadn't she checked on her earlier? Why had she wasted time decorating that tree?

Her baby rubbed against her neck, fussing, and then lay still again, limp. "Opal!"

Startled, and then another weak cry.

Cat didn't bother with a coat. She grabbed her purse and ran outside, hoping the cold air would stop the raging fever in her daughter. She unsnapped the onesie and fluttered the neckline, trying to cool her.

In minutes, her mother pulled into the drive. "What are you doing? Get in the back seat."

"I'm trying to cool her down." Cat didn't recognize her shrill voice.

"Did you take her temp?"

"No."

"You can take it on the way to the doctor's office. Let's go!"

Cat slid into the back seat and lay Opal down. She then fished the thermometer out of the diaper bag and stuck it under Opal's arm and waited. "Mom, please hurry."

"I'm driving as fast as I can in these conditions."

Cat blocked the scary sounds of sloppy snow and slush slapping under the car's tires. Her mom had all-wheel drive. She checked Opal's temperature. "Close to 102, and that's under the arm, so you know it's really higher than that."

"I'm heading straight for the ER."

"That's twenty minutes away."

"We'll make it in fifteen." Her mother sped up as she took a curve, causing the back of her car to fishtail before straightening out.

Cat opened the window, letting cold air blow in over the baby.

Opal's eyes fluttered against the wind, but otherwise she didn't move.

"Call Simon," her mom said.

"I can't." Tears ran down Cat's cheeks. She couldn't bear scaring him or, worse, hearing blame in his voice. "Not yet."

This was her fault, dragging Opal back and forth in the cold every day. Maybe it had been the crowds in town for the shoppers' walk. They'd been crammed on that carriage ride.

"Cat!"

"Not now, Mom. Just drive." Cat rolled Opal onto her side like she did before and stroked her baby's back. Bone-dry and hot. The fever hadn't broken. Not even with the cold air. This was not good.

It seemed like a lifetime before they pulled up to the emergency entrance of the hospital. Cat scooped Opal up and ran inside, leaving her mom to take care of the car.

"My daughter had a seizure and she's limp and feverish," Cat shouted at anyone who would listen.

A woman behind the counter handed her a clipboard. "We need your information with insurance."

"I don't have time for that!"

"Ma'am. The doctors need the information. They'll be with you soon."

Cat shifted Opal so she could take the clipboard and started filling out the trillion questions listed with shaking fingers.

"Ma'am, can you step aside?"

Cat turned to see someone behind her, holding their arm, and Cat growled back, "I have a sick infant, please hurry!"

The receptionist gave her an encouraging smile.

Cat sat down and wrote furiously fast before handing back the clipboard. She knew it had been minutes, but it seemed like hours. She paced the waiting room, rubbing Opal's back when her mother came in from parking the car.

"Anything?" her mom asked.

"Still waiting!" Cat paced some more.

Finally, a nurse called them back and the ER staff went into action, whisking Opal away and ushering Cat alongside.

"Is she okay? Please, tell me she's going to be okay." Desperate questions that no one answered.

"Tell me what happened." A man with a doctor's name tag touched her arm.

Cat closed her eyes and recounted Opal's seizure, reliving the moment with terrible clarity. "I shouldn't have taken her out in the cold. Last night she was cranky, but no temp. I didn't know she was sick…"

"Did she have her two-month shots?"

"Yes."

The doctor looked relieved as he quietly took Opal's vitals and then barked out quick orders for a full workup. Whatever that meant.

Cat started to pray but stopped as a frightening thought took hold of her and wouldn't let go. What if God was finally punishing her?

Simon opened the vault and pulled out the plastic bag with the raw opals he'd purchased with Cat. He should make something special out of the largest one for her for Christmas. He imagined a ring. It was what Cat's parents wanted, what they expected. What did Cat want?

The bell on his front door rang, scattering his thoughts. Someone was in the store.

Heading toward the front of his shop, he spotted a tall woman with her back toward him. She had dull blond hair, which was pulled into a ponytail at the base of her neck. She was looking at a display of local Petoskey-stone and Leland-bluestone jewelry.

"Is there something I can pull out for you to see up close?" Simon asked.

The woman turned. "I'd love to see the bracelets."

She looked familiar, really familiar. "I'm sorry, have we met?"

Recognition registered across her face too. "You were with Cat. Simon, is it? Her husband?"

"Uh, no." After last night's embrace and this morning's breakfast with Cat's father, admitting such a thing seemed wholly inadequate and incomplete.

Simon remembered this woman from the tree lighting

and the hot-chocolate stand. She had made Cat uncomfortable. He extended his hand. "Simon Roberts. And you are?"

She returned the handshake. "Sue Jensen. I've been meaning to come into your shop for ages. How are you and Cat?"

She seemed awfully interested in Cat's welfare. "Fine."

"It's good to see her back home, in Maple Springs." Sue smiled.

"Yes." He was definitely missing something here.

"And so blessed to see her with a baby."

What an odd statement for someone to make. Tipping his head, he pushed a little. "Why's that?"

The woman shook her head and gave an awkward-sounding laugh. "Simply a beautiful baby, is all. Well, I'll have a look at those Petoskey-stone bracelets."

He pulled them out from behind the glass case. He waited as she reviewed each bracelet, hoping she'd elaborate on what she'd said about Opal.

She didn't.

Finally, he asked, "See anything you like?"

The woman closed her eyes a moment as if gathering strength or courage, and then she whispered, "I'm sorry. Another time, perhaps."

"Another time." How had he upset her? This was why he had to get out of dealing with the customers.

A whistle sounded from the woman's purse. She pulled out a phone and read whatever had alerted her with a deep frown. She then surprised him by grabbing hold of his hand. "I'm so sorry about your baby. She'll be fine. God intervenes."

His gut turned at the earnestness in the woman's eyes. "What are you talking about?"

She looked surprised. "Opal's in the hospital with a high fever."

His mouth dropped open when she showed him a prayer-chain text that had come from Helen Zelinsky. His head spun. "I'm sorry, I have to go. I need to close the store, if you'll please leave."

"Of course." The woman looked even more rattled as he held the door for her.

He pulled his cell phone from his pocket and dialed Cat's number, but it went to voice mail. Disconnecting, he searched for Cat's mother's when his phone buzzed. "Hello?"

"Simon? It's Helen—"

He interrupted her, "What's going on with Opal?"

A brief pause on her end. "We're at the emergency room with Opal. Please come."

His stomach lurched. "What happened?"

"Opal's fever spiked and she had a seizure. I'm sorry, but I've got to go." Helen disconnected before he could learn anything more.

Time and space seemed to implode. A seizure sounded serious, like a lifetime ahead with chronic problems and doctors.

No...

Shutting off the lights and setting the alarm, Simon locked up his shop. Then he dashed toward the back alley, where he'd parked, jumped in his car and took off. Fighting terrible thoughts, Simon prayed. He prayed hard.

Time in the ER passed in a blur for Cat. Her mom supported her by helping to hold Opal while the doctors and nurses poked and prodded her baby for bloodwork and cultures. Hearing Opal cry and seeing the blood drawn,

Cat had never felt so helpless. There was nothing she could do to make it better.

She suddenly heard Simon's loud, angry voice out front, demanding information about his daughter.

"Mom, can you go to him?"

Her mother touched her arm. "Will you be okay?"

She nodded, hoping that was true. What if Opal didn't make it? She closed her eyes and tried to shut off the terrible thoughts that plagued her. The fear of a life for a life.

"Hang in there, okay?" One of the ER nurses rubbed her back.

"Thanks." Cat appreciated the compassion and calmed down a little.

As seriously as the staff took Opal's condition, it didn't appear that anyone feared for her baby's life. The doctor had explained that if this were life-threatening, Opal would be transferred downstate instead of upstairs to the pediatric unit.

By the time they transferred Opal up to her room in pediatrics, she was hooked up to an IV of antibiotics in her little hand that had been covered with a sock.

Opal looked terribly small and weak in a hospital crib.

Simon had joined them in the trek upstairs, but he hadn't said a word. His face darkly grim, angry and adrift. Maybe he too prepared for the worst.

Cat traced the tape that held the tiny IV tube in place on her baby's arm and whispered, "I'm so sorry."

Simon glanced at her but said nothing. He returned his focus to their baby.

Opal slept the whole way to the pediatrics unit, no doubt exhausted from crying. She'd wailed through the blood tests and needle pokes with bloodcurdling baby screeches that racked her little body and shredded Cat's heart.

Opal looked lifeless again, limp and defenseless.

"I'm going for coffee and to call your father. Want anything, either of you?" her mom asked.

"I'm fine." Simon's voice sounded raw.

Cat shook her head and slipped into a chair in the corner. Her body shook, so she pulled her knees up to her chest in an attempt to stop the tremors. Memories of paramedics checking the small body of a toddler jumbled with images of the doctors and nurses who had prodded Opal. The two little girls blended into one.

She covered her ears at the memory of Sue Jensen's screams as she relived Opal's cries from moments ago. She felt helpless, just as she had then, a feeling she'd never wanted to feel again.

"Cat!"

She looked up into Simon's worried face. "It's my fault."

He grabbed her shoulders and gave her a gentle shake. "You didn't do anything wrong. Babies get sick. They get fevers."

Cat shook off his touch. "I should have waited another month before taking her out in public. I should have been more careful, instead of taking her back and forth to your jewelry store."

His face had hardened. "Why didn't you call me?"

"I— Uh…" Cat closed her eyes.

"Do you know how I found out? That woman, Sue Jensen, was in my shop when she got a text for prayer from your mom."

She held up her hand in an attempt to deflect his anger, but it rained over her as piercing as physical blows.

"Why didn't you bother to call me?"

"I know I should have. I was…"

"You were determined to keep Opal from me from the

moment you found out you were expecting, and now this. What's going on with you? I'm her father. I have a right to know. What else haven't you told me?"

Squeezing her knees harder against her chest, she looked up into his eyes. "I'll tell you what's going on with me. It's been going on with me for years. My neighbor's three-year-old drowned while I was babysitting her, Simon. Three years old!"

He jerked back as if she'd slapped him.

"I probably should have told you sooner, but how do you tell someone something like that?"

"How old were you?"

Once started, she couldn't stop. As if she had no power over the words falling from her mouth, Cat rambled on. "Sixteen. Old enough to know better, but I wanted to lie in the sun and so I set up toys for her to play with by the shore. She loved the sand. I closed my eyes for a couple of minutes, and then when I opened them, she was gone. She'd walked out on the dock and had fallen in the lake. I tried to revive her, but couldn't. I was too late. I was not paying attention. I was—"

"Did you fall asleep?" He looked horrified.

Cat shook her head. "No. I was listening to the radio, singing along. I never heard the splash."

He bent his head and rubbed his forehead as if he could scrub away the scene she'd described.

She knew he couldn't. Something like that never went away.

"I wasn't paying close enough attention to Opal either. This morning, after you'd gone, she went down for a nap after eating and I finished decorating the tree. I should have checked on her earlier. Maybe I could have caught the fever in time and done something before that seizure."

This time Simon held up his hand and muttered, "Stop."

She couldn't. "Don't you see? I'm not meant to be a mom. I'm not fit for it and God's finally punishing me. If something happens to Opal—"

"Stop it, Catherine." His voice sliced her in two.

She took a breath but kept going. "You need to hear this so you'll know who I am. I destroyed an entire family by being careless. I can't do that again. I can't do that to Opal, to you—" Her voice cracked.

"Stop it!" Simon stood, his face ashen. "It's just a fever."

"We can complete that paternity form. It's in my purse. Maybe…maybe you should be the one to care for her, to take custody. You and my mom. She'll be safer that way. I'll go back to New York and—" She choked on a sob.

He backed away from her as if she'd gone crazy.

"Don't you get it? I failed to protect her. She had a seizure and it could be serious."

Simon stared at her a moment longer and then shook his head and turned away.

Cat watched as Simon kissed his fingers and then leaned over the crib to touch them to Opal's forehead. That gentle gesture broke her in two.

Keeping his hand on their daughter's head, Simon stayed by Opal's bed only a few more moments, head bowed, and then he left without looking back.

She didn't blame him for leaving her. She deserved it. The freedom of finally unloading everything she'd kept secret left her light-headed, so she slumped down into the chair.

The door opened. Her mother had returned. "Cat, honey? What did you say to Simon?"

She looked at her and shrugged. "Everything. He finally knows everything."

Cat had been chasing Christmas wishes, thinking she could make a family with Simon. Like tinsel on artificial trees, Cat's dream that her wishes could come true had been fake too. A false hope.

The only thing she knew for certain was her love for Opal was real. She'd rather give her up than harm her in any way. She'd fallen for Simon too, and that was why she should let them both go.

Returning to New York might be better for everyone. She could get her old job back and her old life of being responsible for no one but herself. No one else should have to pay the price for her carelessness.

Chapter Thirteen

Simon walked into the hallway as if coming up for air. While he'd paced in the ER, Helen had told him that all Opal's tests were merely to rule out anything serious. She'd said that the emergency room doctor believed the odds were in his baby girl's favor.

Cat's mom had been through similar scares with her own children, so he'd relaxed some. Helen had also mentioned that Opal had received her two-month immunization shots in New York, before Cat had moved home, though Cat hadn't yet found a pediatric doctor in Maple Springs. The knowledge that Opal had the protection of the vaccinations was comforting, as well.

The seizure still worried him. What if Cat was right and it turned serious? How long would it take for something to show up on those tests?

"Hey, man, you okay?" Cat's brother Zach slapped him on the back.

Simon blew out his breath. "I don't know."

"My mother says a high fever in infants is not uncommon."

"I know, but Cat—" Simon stopped.

He still reeled from the things Cat had told him. The

loss of a child under her care was horrific, even if it had been accidental. Still, her admission made him rethink everything he knew about her and blew apart what tenuous trust he had.

He'd trusted her enough to share his painful past and yet she hadn't returned the favor until today. She'd kept yet another bombshell from him. What cut the deepest was she hadn't called him about Opal. He'd had to find out from a stranger that his daughter was sick and in the hospital.

"Come on. Let's go down to the cafeteria."

"I'm not hungry." He felt sick to his stomach.

"I am. Come on."

Simon walked silently alongside Zach, his mind numb.

"How's Cat holding up?" Zach asked.

"She's a mess."

Zach nodded. "She's scared, Simon. Ever since she was sixteen, Cat has always been afraid of herself."

That statement pierced hot and then cold. Cold enough for him to shiver. Cold enough to wonder if perhaps he shouldn't take Cat up on her offer to take custody of Opal.

Cat may have uttered sheer nonsense in the heat of the moment, but Simon wasn't too keen on the idea of Opal growing up afraid of her mother's issues. Cat had a way of curling into herself when something bad happened and now he knew why. Another accident might send her over the edge, never to return, and then what?

Simon knew all too well what it was like tiptoeing around an unstable parent. He'd never had a father who might have balanced things out. But then, his father also could have made things much worse.

What would he be for Opal?

More ice-laced fear shot through him, but he knew he

had to give Opal his all. As Cat had said, truly providing for her would take more than money.

He and Zach walked the rest of the way in silence, each with his own thoughts. When they finally reached the cafeteria, Zach ordered a sandwich and Simon bought a soda. Choosing an isolated table, Simon sat down and waited for Zach to finish eating.

"She told me about the drowning," he finally said.

Zach leaned back in his chair. "I was home on leave when it happened. The first responders ruled it an accidental death, but that didn't matter to Cat. Muriel Jensen hadn't been under the water very long and Cat had tried in vain to revive the little girl with CPR and mouth-to-mouth. Seeing the devastation in her eyes is something I'll never forget."

Simon winced.

"Muriel had been the youngest. I think they had a couple more kids afterward, though. They still go to my folks' church."

Simon rubbed his forehead, remembering Sue Jensen in his shop and the intensity of her gaze. It was small wonder that Cat had been uncomfortable around the woman. "She came into my shop today, right before your mom called me from the ER."

"They're a nice family. They never blamed her, but Cat still blames herself." Zach shrugged before continuing. "Even with counseling, she never babysat again. She wouldn't even look after our little sister and brother."

Simon considered his friend's words. Of course, Cat blamed herself—a natural reaction. Her fear of somehow hurting Opal because of carelessness might be natural too.

What wasn't natural or acceptable was Cat believing she was somehow bad for Opal, or that Opal was better off without her. She'd been ready to relinquish the baby to his care after one fever. He'd almost followed her reasoning, and that was crazy. Opal needed Cat. Far more than Opal needed him.

Cat might go through this every time Opal got hurt. He'd never forget the wild look Cat had in her eyes the day Opal had rolled off the couch. Zach's words made sense. Cat was not only afraid of herself, she was scared of motherhood. Scared of making a mistake. Another deadly one.

Simon stood, antsy to get back to Opal's room before the doctor returned with news. Opal's welfare was his primary concern, so he made his way back to the pediatric unit with his thoughts in a tangle.

He wasn't sure how to handle what Cat had done, both past and present. Even though he believed what had happened with that Jensen girl had been an accident, what doubts might rise to the surface every time Opal took a tumble? Would he look for fault in Cat every time? Would he be able to stop her from looking for fault in herself?

That was no way to live and certainly no way to have a relationship. He wasn't sure he could trust her…and it seemed as though she still wasn't ready to trust him. Cat hadn't called him when Opal was at her most vulnerable, and Simon wasn't sure he could forgive her for that.

Cat looked up when Simon returned. He seemed more remote than ever. Without even one glance her way, he sat in the chair next to Opal's crib. He reached over the lowered side and held their daughter's hand. The one free of the IV.

Cat looked away. Whatever they might have had was gone.

Her mom got up and brushed back Cat's hair. "I'm going to run home and get your father. He made reservations at a hotel nearby, so I'll bring back an overnight bag for you. Call me if anything changes, okay?"

"Okay. Grab a couple of those bottles in the fridge, and my laptop. Please." She had no idea if she'd be able to feed Opal well enough.

The nurse said the fever had come down some, yet Opal still slept hard, looking much too lifeless. They had Wi-Fi here, and Cat wanted to research these fever procedures as much as possible on a bigger screen than her phone.

"It'll be okay, honey. Opal is a healthy baby. She'll pull through," her mother whispered.

"I hope so." As long as those cultures came back negative, they'd be okay. But they wouldn't know those results for a couple of days. Her bloodwork was quicker, but they hadn't heard anything yet on that.

Her mother gave her a pointed look toward Simon.

Cat drew her legs up against her chest, wrapping the blanket she'd grabbed from the adult bed around herself. There wasn't much else to say. He knew all about her now and it was obvious that he didn't want anything more to do with her.

Her mother patted her arm and left.

Cat stared out the window at the snowflakes falling gently from the sky. Opal's room faced west, where the sun had dipped low, behind a mountain of clouds, turning the horizon pink and darker purple. It'd be dark soon.

She needed to feed Opal, even though her body drew in on itself, empty. Like her.

Closing her eyes, Cat uttered a silent prayer, *Dear Lord, please heal Opal. Punish me, not her. I'll give up anything, everything, if You'll make her well.*

The sound of Opal's breathing echoed in her ears. She labored as if her nose might be stuffed. If only this might be nothing more than a common cold, but would a simple cold cause such a high fever and seizure?

Minutes went by and silence still stretched between her and Simon.

"Zach told me about the Jensen girl, how you tried hard to save her." Simon's voice was soft and low, but it still sounded too loud in the quiet room. "It wasn't your fault, Cat. An accident."

Cat locked on to Simon's gaze. "Does that matter? I could have prevented that accident. I could have made sure she didn't go near the dock. I could have kept her inside. I could have paid better attention."

"You were only sixteen." He looked at her now, but the anger remained in his eyes. The disappointment.

"Old enough to know the danger of small kids around a lake."

"You've got to let it go. Opal needs you, so you might as well drop the idea of giving her up. Living in the past won't help her future."

Cat stared at him. He was one to talk about letting the past dictate choices. But then, he was right about Opal needing her. Could she really leave her own daughter? "What about our future?"

Simon didn't say anything. He didn't have to.

She'd lost him. "Have you ever wished with all your might that you could do one thing over? Given one moment in time to repeat something differently."

He nodded. "After my mother kicked me out, I was angry and hurt and I never went back. I never checked on my sister or brother until they were taken by child protective services. Even though I took them in, the damage was done. I'd already left them once, so they never trusted me again."

"You can't blame yourself for their choices."

He didn't look like he believed her. "It wasn't their choice when I left."

Just like she'd taken his choice away by not telling him about Opal.

"When were you going to tell me all this? *Any* of this?"

Cat looked down at her clasped hands. He had every right to be angry. "I tried to tell you about Muriel Jensen last night, but then…" She couldn't bear to revisit the kisses they'd shared. "Opal fussed. She was sick and I didn't even realize it."

"Why didn't *you* call me today?"

The door opened and the doctor came in and introduced himself.

She and Simon both met him at the end of Opal's crib and shook the man's hand. Standing close, they listened as the doctor went over the protocol of treating an infant with a fever-induced seizure.

"Her bloodwork looks good, but that temp is still higher than I like to see. We'll keep her tonight as a precaution and see how she does tomorrow."

Weak with relief, Cat nearly crumpled, but Simon supported her with a strong arm around her waist. As she listened to the doctor's encouragement as he stated that he believed Opal's illness would prove to be a virus, Cat's eyes blurred.

"Thank you." Simon shook the man's hand again before the doctor left. Then he turned to her. "Have you eaten anything today?"

Cat tried to remember. She'd had a piece of toast and tea at Simon's house when she couldn't find coffee. "Not really, no."

"Go eat something. I'll stay with Opal." He turned away from her, dismissing her like he'd done that morning when he'd put her on the small plane.

Cat wanted to reach out to him but caressed her baby's face instead. Opal looked peaceful, even though her forehead still felt warm. "I have my cell. Call me if she wakes. She hasn't eaten much today either."

"I will."

At the door, Cat turned. "I'm sorry I didn't tell you everything sooner."

"What did you think I'd do?"

Cat shrugged, unable to speak through the tightness in her throat. She had feared it would push him away from her—like it had now.

"I don't know what to tell you," she whispered.

He looked through her. "Go eat, Cat."

She stepped out of the hospital room, knowing she'd lost something precious. She'd lost Simon's regard, his trust. There was no way she'd gain his love, not now that he knew the terrible things she'd done.

Cat texted her mother the results from the bloodwork before making her way down the hall. She spotted her brother in the waiting room, watching the evening news. "You're still here?"

"Yeah, how is she?" He opened his arms.

She went right into them, welcoming the bear hug. "The doctor thinks it's a virus, since her bloodwork came back good, but the fever's still there, so he'd like her to stay overnight and we'll see tomorrow."

"That's good. You're staying here too, then?"

Cat nodded. "Mom's getting my stuff and coming back with Dad. You don't have to stay."

"How's Simon?"

Cat shrugged. "He's with Opal."

"I'll peek in before leaving."

"Thank you." Cat's eyes burned. "For being a friend to him."

"Sure thing." Zach looked concerned. "You guys okay?"

"I don't think so." Cat gave her brother a weak smile and left before she broke down and cried.

She should have trusted Simon with the truth earlier. She should have trusted him long ago by telling him when she'd found out she was pregnant.

In the cafeteria, Cat ordered a turkey club and a glass of milk. She might not be hungry, but she'd eat. For Opal's sake, she had to relax somehow so she'd be able to feed her daughter when she awoke. Opal still didn't take a bottle well.

Gazing out over the view of Lake Michigan and the lights of Maple Springs shining from across the bay, Cat considered her prayer. God was healing Opal. She'd made a deal. He was delivering on His end. Maybe losing Simon was part of that deal. A deal she had to accept.

"Cat?"

She looked up into Sue Jensen's anxious face. What was she doing here?

"How is Opal?"

"Better. The doctor thinks it's viral."

"Good. I'm on the church prayer chain. I thought I'd come to the cafeteria to see if you came down, in case you needed a little extra support."

That was kind of her. Beyond kind, maybe, but really, why?

Cat stood. She'd wrap up her food and take it with her. "I should get back to her."

Sue touched her arm, her expression tense and uncertain but filled with compassion. "You've got to let Muriel go."

"I can't." Tears filled Cat's eyes. "It was my fault."

Sue grabbed both her hands. "I should have warned

you that I'd caught her sneaking out onto the dock that very morning, but we were in a hurry to leave that day and I failed to mention it."

Cat pulled her hands back. She'd heard Sue say this before, but something in her tone right now made Cat pause. She'd heard the desperation in Sue's voice before, but not the self-incrimination. It hadn't mattered because Cat had been the one at fault. No matter what Sue said, she should have known better.

"You can live without the guilt," Sue said softly.

Cat sat back down. "How?"

Sue sat right next to her. "Give it to God."

Talk about cliché. Cat ran her hand over her forehead. "I've tried. It hasn't worked."

"You have to believe He'll take it, Cat. Give your guilt to God before it gets in the way of how you treat Opal."

Hours ago, she'd offered to leave Opal because she couldn't handle the thought of losing her or causing her harm.

"You've been heavy on my heart for weeks," Sue continued. "Even before you came home. You're a mom now and it's a frightening job, but if you let fear rule, it won't be good for you or her. Or your fellow, Simon."

"Simon?" Cat recalled the angry look on his face. She'd already done the damage there.

"I've seen you with your daughter, Cat. You're a good mother. You were a good babysitter too. The best I ever had. What happened was a horrible accident. Don't punish your daughter or Simon by emotionally whipping yourself. God doesn't seek your punishment, He seeks your trust. Accept His grace, His forgiveness, and allow yourself to forgive *you*."

Tears ran down Cat's face as those words finally sank

in with a different clarity than before. For years, she'd expected punishment from God and she'd run from Him.

When she'd found out she was pregnant, she'd feared God's justice even more. She'd offered herself up to God as payment, praying that he'd keep Opal safe, as if making some kind of deal would work. When had she ever truly trusted God's love or His grace without trying to turn it into a bargain? She'd muddled through by her own merit, on her own strength, her own will.

Not my will but Thine.

"But it still hurts," Cat whispered.

"It does. The hurt remains, but God will be there in the pain. Use it to draw closer to Him. Rely on Him, Cat. It's the only way to truly live again."

"But I don't deserve it. I don't deserve forgiveness."

Sue gathered up her hands again and squeezed. "None of us do and yet God sent His son to die on the cross, taking on all our sins. Refusing to accept your own forgiveness is like slapping what He did down as unnecessary."

Cat hadn't considered it that way. She'd never truly surrendered her life or her heart. She'd held back. "I want to forgive."

"Then let's do it. Now." Sue grabbed her hands, bowed her head and prayed.

Cat prayed with her. Instead of begging or making promises or deals, Cat simply asked. She envisioned her guilt on a silver platter and offered it to God, trusting that He'd finally take it from her because, this time, she'd let go.

Tears streamed down her face as she hugged Sue Jensen, a woman she'd be wise to learn more from. "Thank you."

Sue returned her embrace. "Eat now, regain your

strength and then go to Opal. We'll see each other again soon. Okay?"

"I'd like that." Cat sniffed as she gave Sue's hand one last squeeze. "Thank you for coming here, for helping."

Sue nodded, her eyes shiny. "We can help each other."

Cat watched the woman leave and then focused on her plate. She ate everything because it was something she had to do for her daughter's sake. Refusing to revisit the guilt so soon after she'd given it away was also something she'd do for Opal.

And Simon.

She balled her hands into fists. Whether or not they had a future would not stop her from working with him to be good parents. From here on out, she'd be honest with him. Upfront. Unafraid.

Walking back to Opal's room, Cat experienced a renewed sense of peace. She was forgiven. It was time to not only accept that, but live as if she truly believed it. With God's grace, she had hope for the future. One where she'd have joy, even carrying the pain of her past.

Chapter Fourteen

Opal woke up with a start and her little body jerked.

"Hey, Princess." Simon caressed his daughter's cheek. She still felt warm to the touch, but not overly so. He'd have never guessed she had a fever.

She looked at him, wide-eyed, scrunched up her face and cried. She howled like she had that first time he'd held her.

He ignored sudden panic and picked her up, taking care not to dislodge the sock covering the tiny IV in her left hand.

She quieted somewhat, rubbed her face into his shoulder and then cried some more, only louder.

The door opened and Cat rushed inside. "Is she okay?"

"She wants you." Simon carefully handed the baby over but remained close, making sure the IV tube reached. It did.

"I'm here, Opal. Mommy will always be here for you." Cat cuddled their daughter. Then she looked at him, expectantly, as if asking whether or not he'd be here for Opal too.

Simon didn't want to make the same mistakes with his daughter that he'd made with his siblings. How was he supposed to avoid that? He'd thought getting close to people was the problem—but perhaps he'd created more problems by pushing people away.

Opal quieted and rubbed her face against Cat.

"She's hungry. Will you hand me the diaper bag?"

He handed over the diaper bag and then backed away as Opal let loose another impatient howl. That had to be a good sign that she felt better.

Cat covered herself and the baby with the small fleece blanket. "Simon?"

At the door he turned. "Yes?"

"I'm sorry for not calling you about Opal. I should have called you on the way to the ER."

"Why didn't you?"

"I was a little crazy and afraid you'd blame me."

The truth in her eyes hit him hard. "What have I done to make you fear my reaction?"

She shook her head. "Nothing. Nothing at all."

Simon nodded, finally understanding. It had been her hang-ups making that decision. He exited the room and nearly ran into a nurse. "Ah, she's feeding the baby now."

"That's wonderful news." The nurse smiled. "I'm going in to check her vitals."

Simon waited in the hall. Slamming his hands into the deep pockets of the khakis he wore, he closed his eyes. He didn't know what to pray, so he merely whispered, "God, you know what we need. What I need."

Seconds turned into minutes and still the nurse hadn't exited the room. Antsy to get back in there, Simon opened his eyes and stared at the wall across from him.

Whosoever shall seek to save his life shall lose it; and whosoever shall lose his life shall preserve it.

The scripture passage came to mind once again, hauntingly so. He'd tried to make it fit what he wanted to do, but he'd never been fully satisfied with that explanation. He still wanted to gem hunt, it was part of what he did for a living, but that was not what the passage had meant.

He flushed as if he might pass out, but he wasn't light-headed and this had nothing to do with dizziness. Simon was hearing from God, deep in his spirit, and he finally understood the text. Simon had spent most of his adult life trying to protect himself from emotional hurt. Closing himself off was no way to live.

Cat had let him down. No, more than that, she'd betrayed him by keeping Opal a secret. And then she'd deeply hurt him by not turning to him when Opal was sick. He'd felt rejection like nothing he'd ever experienced before.

She'd called her mom instead of him—should he really hold that against her? He shouldn't. It was not reason enough to keep from forgiving her.

Loving Cat meant losing his life a little, day by day. Year by year. Preserving his life meant living for more than himself.

"Everything okay?" Andy Zelinsky laid a hand on his arm.

Simon nearly jumped. He looked into the concerned face of Cat's parents. "She's feeding the baby and the nurse is in there now."

Helen didn't wait and entered the room without a word.

Andy nodded. "Have you eaten dinner?"

Why did everyone worry about food at times like these? Simon shook his head. "No."

"We can hit the cafeteria after you hear." Cat's father leaned against the wall and waited with him.

After a few minutes, he added, "These things never get easy, waiting out a child's illness."

Simon looked at him. "How'd you manage ten kids? Did anyone ever get hurt?"

Andy laughed. "Of course they did. We've seen our share of broken bones and stitches. Cat suffered a concussion from falling out of a tree when she was ten."

"Somehow that doesn't surprise me." Simon smiled at the thought of a ten-year-old Cat climbing trees. She'd been an adventurer even then.

"A parent's concern doesn't stop once their kids are grown either. It was difficult every time Zach was deployed. Helen and I worried when Cat traveled to all those remote places. Matthew's time off for Christmas has been delayed yet another week. He's out on the Great Lakes right now and has seen some terrible weather."

Simon thought about Cat's fears and realized they were not so crazy. "How do you stand it?"

Andy smiled. "Like I said at breakfast, you pray for them daily, but ultimately you hand them over to God. No matter what happens in life, God is God and He'll be with you in good times and bad. You're never alone."

Simon read the deep conviction in the man's eyes and knew he didn't speak lightly. Grateful for Andy's wisdom and his presence, Simon waited alongside him, and when the door finally opened and the nurse exited with a smile, Simon let out a deep breath.

"Go on in," Andy told him. "I'll wait for you here."

"Thanks, Andy. For everything." Simon stepped back into Opal's room and his gaze immediately sought Cat's.

She held Opal in her arms.

"How is she?"

"Much better. Her temp is normal. And her vitals are all good. She ate well too."

Words escaped him, so he nodded.

"I'll let Andy know," Helen whispered and left.

Simon hadn't looked away from Cat, but still he had no words. He had to forgive her and move on.

"The nurse said the doctor will come back in the morning and, as long as she continues to improve, we should be good to go home."

Home.

The desire to have Cat and Opal home with him hit hard. To really have life, he'd need to give his away. "That's good."

Cat gazed at Opal another moment before looking back at him. "Are you okay?"

"Better now, I think." There was so much to say, but he didn't know where to start. For now, he simply wanted to hold Cat, which wouldn't be easy when she sat in a hospital chair, careful to keep Opal's left hand free.

"You should go with my parents to the cafeteria and eat something. You look terrible."

He took a few steps until he crouched before her. "Are you okay?"

"Better now, I think." She copied his words.

He laughed softly. "Because the fever's gone?"

"That and I talked to Sue Jensen when I was in the cafeteria. She heard about Opal from the church prayer line and so she came looking for me."

"That's how I found out about Opal. And then your mom called."

Cat touched his arm. "Simon, I'm sorry."

He covered her hand with his. He chose to forgive. "Me too, Catherine."

Her fingers dug deep. "She told me to give my guilt to God. The only way to live with such regret is to trust that God can make things right in my soul."

Simon felt those words fit for him too. "Are we going to do that, then? Trust Him?"

"I want to."

"I want us both to be whole." There were things he needed to know, things they needed to say, but not now. For now, he'd let them go. He'd believe Sue Jensen's words and trust that God could make things right.

In both of them.

Cat woke and checked on Opal. Her baby looked peaceful, swaddled in a soft cotton blanket. Her little left arm with the sock-covered IV rested on her rounded little belly. Cat reached over and touched Opal's forehead. Normal.

Cat felt more normal too, now that she'd finally forgiven herself—and now that Simon knew the truth about her. With his help, Cat had pulled the adult hospital bed right next to the crib. She slipped off that bed, taking the blanket with her and wrapping it around her shoulders. She padded quietly to the window and looked back, making sure she hadn't disturbed Simon.

He snoozed in a semi-reclining sort of chair in the corner, half covered by a cotton blanket that matched hers. His dark hair was messy, his face unshaven and his white shirt wrinkled. This was how he'd looked when they'd first met. He had stayed with her all night in the hospital. He could have gone home, but he'd stayed.

Her parents were close by as well, staying overnight at a hotel only minutes away. Her loved ones had rallied around her when she'd needed them most.

Even Sue Jensen. Especially Sue Jensen.

Cat might always fight the temptation of giving in to guilt, but at least she'd accepted that God wasn't out to punish her. She knew deep down that He wanted to love her and He wanted her love in return, free from fear.

Love.

She wanted to love Opal without fear. Simon too. Was it possible? Could she truly trust the Lord enough to cast out those fears?

Gazing at the clear dark sky with a swath of stars and a sliver of bright moon hanging low in the sky, Cat finally felt at peace, but something still stirred deep within her. The pain was there. Sure, the memories of that awful day remained as clear as if it had happened yesterday. It would always be with her, a part of her. If only she could pour some of that out somehow.

Glancing at Simon, she slowly pulled her laptop from its case, cringing when the plug hit the floor with a thwack. Holding her breath, she waited, but he didn't move. His breathing remained deep and even.

She opened the lid and powered up, and then she stared at the screen. Her fingers poised over the keys, Cat started with the stark truth.

I accidentally killed a three-year-old girl...

Praying that God would loosen what she'd secretly gripped so tightly, Cat was amazed as the story flew from her heart through her fingers onto the computer screen. She didn't hold anything back, no whitewashing or making it pretty. She didn't qualify anything either. She simply retold what happened, and her feelings and reactions flowed out afterward.

She didn't know how long she'd been typing away, but when she finally came to the end, she leaned back, completely spent. Empty yet filled. Tears streamed down her cheeks as she hit Save and then resaved it in the nether regions of her online storage space.

Simon stirred across the room. "What time is it?"

Cat peeked at the time in the bottom corner of her laptop. "Nearly seven."

"Are you okay?" Simon's craggy whisper sounded more dear than she ever thought possible.

She wiped at the tears with her fingers. She was a mess but oddly at peace. She'd rely on God to clear up and organize her body, soul and spirit. Left to her own devices, she merely rearranged the mess, making it bigger. "I think I might be. Finally."

"That's good to hear." He got up and came toward her. "What are you working on? Your freelance article?"

"No." She let out a shuddering breath before closing the lid of her laptop and setting it down on the floor. Maybe she'd let Simon read it, maybe this was for Opal a few years down the road, so she'd understand her mother's issues.

Looking up into Simon's worried eyes, Cat whispered. "I'm working on me."

He pulled her to her feet so he could face her. "I'm working on me too. You scared me pretty good."

"I'm sorry." Cat searched his dark eyes.

He tucked her hair behind her ear. "You made me face how empty I kept my life."

She understood that too. She'd traveled in an attempt to escape her past, but it went with her anyway.

"Being parents is not going to be easy," Simon said. "There's things like this fever that will take us by surprise, things we can't control. I guess that's where trusting God comes in. Ultimately, Opal is in His hands."

Cat searched Simon's eyes. Like his tea, she needed to steep in that wisdom until the truth of it ran dark and strong through her veins. But there was still the question of them. "What about you and me?

"We've got some things to figure out yet, but I need you to know—" He cleared his throat. "Know that I love you, Catherine."

She felt tears well up all over again. "I love you too, Simon."

They leaned close, their lips mere seconds from each other, when the door opened. A new nurse entered. Shift change.

"Oh, sorry, I can come back."

Cat backed up, away from Simon, but she never let go of his hand. "No, please come in and check on our baby, tell us she's better. She feels better."

The nurse was young and she smiled. "I'll have a look, but I'll leave the details to the doctor. He'll be in later this morning."

"Okay." Cat watched her every move, hoping, praying they could go home.

"Cat, look." Simon pointed at the window.

The sky had grown a brilliant pink from the coming sunrise. A new day dawned. For all of them.

Chapter Fifteen

It had been a week since they'd brought Opal home from her stay in the hospital. The cultures had all come back negative of any bacterial growth. Her illness had been viral and the seizure a result of a sudden high fever spike.

His little princess was back to her gurgling self with some added smiles and babbling. Opal now recognized him as soon as he entered a room. She'd bounce up and down like the Christmas bubble lights on the Zelinsky Christmas tree when she spotted him. That small action was more precious to him than anything.

Nearly every day this week after he closed up shop, Simon had driven north of town to Cat's parents'. Cat and Opal had stayed put, not coming by the store until Opal's sickness was gone. He missed having them at the shop—

His cell rang, cutting off his thoughts. He checked the number that belonged to his sister and took a deep breath. "Hello?"

"Simon? It's Margo."

"Thanks for getting back to me so soon."

"I'm glad you called. I didn't know how to get a hold of you and, well, it's been a while." Her voice sounded strained, but not angry.

Relief washed through him. "Since Mom's funeral. Look, I need to apologize for many things, not calling sooner being one of them."

Silence.

"Margo?"

"I'm here. You know there's a lot of blame all around, on all of us." She paused, took a deep breath and continued, "I got your message and, so, yeah, we can make it the weekend before Christmas."

"Great, I'll reserve a room for you and—is it Jim?" Her second husband. Simon remembered meeting him at the funeral and he'd seemed like a nice guy.

"Yes, but I can do it—"

"Margo, let me get this. I owe you a lot more than a couple nights' stay." Simon wanted to do it, and she needed to accept.

"Okay."

"No word on Barry?"

His sister sighed. "No. He won't talk to me. He's out of jail, living somewhere, but I don't know where. He's lost, Simon. Lost to us both."

That kicked him in the gut. "I should have—"

"Stop right there. We've all made choices, some good and some bad. You were trying to help and we didn't give you much in the way of thanks for that."

Simon felt himself smile. Forgiveness seemed to be a contagious thing these days. He looked forward to knowing his sister better. "We can talk more when you're here."

"I look forward to that. See you soon."

"And more often."

"I'd like that."

"Me too." Simon disconnected.

His sister lived in Green Bay, Wisconsin. A six-hour

drive through the Upper Peninsula. He could take Cat and Opal there for a visit one day.

Simon returned to work, polishing the large opal. He'd have it faceted in time. He planned a special setting that would complement the opal's large size. He'd asked Helen if she'd watch the baby this Friday evening. She'd also agreed to open her house—

Simon couldn't get ahead of himself. In two days, he'd take Cat out for dinner. Their first real date. It wouldn't be the last. Not by a long shot, but first, he had to finish the ring.

Cat twirled so the full skirt of the black dress she'd borrowed from her mom fluttered around her knees. Slipping into her clunky black boots, Cat checked the clock. Simon would pick her up any minute.

Tromping down the stairs, Cat spotted Simon in the living room and stopped. He looked elegant, dressed in a dark gray wool suit. "Hello."

His eyes widened when he saw her. "Catherine."

Something about the way he said her full name still sent a thrilling shiver up her spine. "You look nice."

He stepped toward her, never breaking his gaze. "So do you."

Cat's belly did somersaults. She had an idea what he was up to, asking her out to dinner, stating he'd already asked Cat's mom to babysit Opal. She hoped her hunch was correct. "Ready?"

"I'll get our coats."

Cat glanced at her mom. "Call my cell if you need me."

"I won't need you. Now go and enjoy." Her mother grinned and pushed her forward.

This was it. Cat was pretty sure Simon was going to ask her to marry him. *Maybe.* He'd kept his plans for his scheduled gem hunt after the first of the year, but he'd promised to return. He'd be gone only weeks, instead of months.

She'd be busy while he was gone, between the store and her new friendship with Sue Jensen. While Cat holed up at her parents' until Opal recovered, she'd spent some time with Sue. The Jensen family still lived down the road from her folks, in the very same house.

It had been the first time since the drowning that Cat had set foot into that house and it had been rough. She'd let Sue read the journal entry she'd typed in the pre-dawn hours at the hospital, and after they'd both cried, Sue had suggested that Cat publish it somewhere. Simon had agreed, after he'd read it. Something to consider, especially if her experience could somehow help others.

Simon slipped into his wool coat and then held open hers.

She slid her arms into her coat and turned toward her mom. She'd fed Opal before getting ready. "Not sure when we'll be back. If Opal cries, she might take a bottle."

"No worries. You two have a good time." Her mom waved them off.

Cat exited the house, only to stick her head back in. "There are fresh bottles for Opal in the fridge."

"Yes, Cat, I know. Go."

Cat squared her shoulders and stepped off her parents' front porch. She grabbed hold of Simon's arm with a sense of anticipation mixed with dread. This was their first real date. Would he ask her tonight or wait until he returned from Africa?

They entered the Maple Springs Inn and the place was crowded. Christmas music came from someone on a piano in the bar. Thankfully Helen had suggested that he make reservations, else they may not have made it in tonight.

He wanted to do this right and proper, and the Inn was perfect and decorated to the hilt for the holidays. Real Christmas trees graced every dining room. There were only three open to the public this time of year, as the fourth was reserved for private parties.

Passing by one tree festooned with white feathers and crystal, he caught a whiff of pine and remembered gathering greens with Cat. They'd already started toward their lifetime of memories.

The hostess led them to a small table close to a real log-burning fireplace. Holding out a chair for Cat, he patted the box in his suit-coat pocket and nerves shuddered through him.

He loved Cat and he wanted Opal to have both a mom and a dad who were together, forever. He wasn't sure about giving Opal brothers and sisters. But then, they'd figure that out in time. He wanted Cat to join him on the next gem hunt in the fall. Opal would be a year old by then. Old enough to stay with her grandparents for a week. One day, perhaps Opal could go with them too, traveling.

"Isn't this pretty?" Cat sniffed the fresh red rose tucked into a vase with some pine. All the tables had them.

He rubbed the back of his neck. What if she said no? "Yes, very nice."

"You okay?" Cat asked.

"Yes, why?"

She smiled. "You seem, I don't know, nervous or something."

"I am. Look, Cat, I was going to wait until after dinner, but this box is burning a hole in my pocket." He reached for the ring box and set it down in front of her.

Inside was the opal of his dreams. The best of the lot he'd purchased and the best he'd ever seen, anywhere. He'd polished and faceted the raw opal into a near ten-carat engagement ring, cradled in white gold, with a crescent-moon sweep of diamonds along one side.

He hoped Cat liked it.

She took a deep breath. "Should I open it?"

He gave her a look.

She reached for the box, clenched her fingers into fists and then relaxed them by shaking them out.

"Now who's nervous?" he taunted.

She made a face in return. Touching the lid of the black velvet box, her gaze sought his, questioning.

"I hope you like it. If not, I can set something else, something you might prefer."

A worried look crept into her pretty blue eyes. "Is this my Christmas present, because I didn't bring yours with me."

"No, Cat. It's not for Christmas. It's for forever." He took another deep breath while Cat stared at the box. He adjusted his tie, loosening it a tad, unbuttoning the top button of his newly pressed shirt, waiting for her to open the lid.

Finally, she did so with a gasp. "Oh."

"Will you marry me?"

Her fingers shook as she picked up the box and handed it back to him with tears in her eyes.

His stomach rolled over and died. He thought he might black out from the throbbing in his ears and the tearing of his heart. Was this no, then?

"Could you put it on my finger, please?"

He tipped his head. "So, you will?"

She laughed then. "Yes, Simon. I will marry you, if you'll put that gorgeous ring on my finger."

"It's from the group of raw stones I bought with you."
He took her hand in his and felt her tremble. "Why are
you shaking?"

She closed her eyes and one tear tripped out from beneath her lashes to run down her cheek. "I never thought
this was possible for me. To feel, you know, this happy."

Without letting go of her hand, he pulled the ring from
the box and brought it to his lips. He kissed the large opal
before slipping it onto her finger. "We're going to make
it, you and I. We're going to have a happy life raising our
daughter together."

She nodded and another tear escaped.

He let go of her and then stood and pulled his chair
around the small table to sit right next to her. "I've never
loved like this."

Her eyes searched his. "I know, me neither."

Then she held her hand out in front of her. She moved
her fingers so the colors within the opal danced in the
soft glow of the fire. "This ring is amazing. Thank you
for making it for me."

"I think it had your name upon it from the start."

She leaned toward him, gently pulling his head to hers.

He returned the kiss, not caring that they were in the
middle of a crowded restaurant dining room. He'd never
expected to experience the kind of happiness that came
with having a family of his own.

When they finally broke apart, Simon chuckled.
"Maybe I'd best return to my side of the table."

"Nope, you stay right here." Cat smiled up at the waiter
who introduced himself and then offered to rearrange
the place setting.

Simon took the offered menu. Now that they'd gotten
the engagement out of the way, the wedding date came
next and he hoped Cat would agree to what he'd planned

with the help of her mother. "Now that you've agreed to be my wife, let's talk dates."

Cat chuckled. "You're getting right to it."

"I see no reason for delay, do you?"

"No." She covered his hand, looking serious. "The sooner, the better, and nothing big. I'd rather it just be family."

Relieved that she didn't want a grand event, he asked, "What do you think about the Saturday before Christmas?"

Her eyes grew round. "That's like a week away. Where on earth will we find a place?"

"Your mother offered up their house. Your family will be there and mine—well, my sister has agreed to come."

"Oh, Simon, you talked to your sister? That's wonderful. What about your brother?"

"I'm still trying to track him down."

Cat looked thoughtful. "So, you have it all planned."

"Do you mind? I've heard it said that girls like big weddings. This will be pretty tame."

"It'll be perfect. I've never really thought much about my own wedding, so whatever we do is fine. I'd rather plan our honeymoon for when Opal is older. I can think of a couple of places I'd love to show you."

Of course she could.

"I'm in your hands."

He was too. He was trusting her with his heart, his daughter and the rest of his life. Of all the places he'd been and they planned to go, this was where he wanted to be most. Alongside Cat, with her hand in his. Forever.

Epilogue

Cat spent the morning of her wedding day helping her mother. The last item on the list was a quick arrangement of the dozens of red poinsettias in the family room. Her mother wanted to line a path with the velvety plants down the stairs to where she'd meet Simon in front of the fireplace. "Where did you get all these?"

"This close to Christmas, they were on sale." Her mom grinned.

"Nicely done." Cat looked everything over with a critical eye, but not a single thing seemed out of place.

Her parents' home made the perfect setting for a Christmas wedding, with the tall Christmas tree covered in twinkling white and bubble lights and special ornaments collected or handmade through the years.

They had moved the furniture out to make room for the rented white wedding chairs and square tables that were scattered throughout the room. Each table had a smaller potted poinsettia as a centerpiece. The reception would be held here as well, with a list of attendees that was barely larger than a regular Zelinsky family dinner.

Cat considered how much of her life had been spent trying to escape this house, along with the memories it held, but today she knew her past wouldn't overshadow her wedding day. Sue Jensen and her husband had not only accepted the wedding invitation, but had brought along a basket of baked goods that graced the loaded dessert table.

Her mom rubbed her back. "You okay?"

Cat nodded with confidence. "I am. Everything is perfect, Mom. Thank you."

Her mom smiled and then quickly checked her watch. "You'd better get ready. It won't be long before everyone's here. I'm going to check on your father and make sure he's putting on the suit I picked out."

Cat gave her mom's hand a squeeze before she left.

The minister from Simon's church, now hers as well, would soon marry them in front of her family and Simon's. Cat had met his sister, Margo, and her husband the night before. She liked them and looked forward to visiting them as Simon promised.

"Hey, Cat, shouldn't you get dressed?" Her brother Cam had arrived, taking over kitchen duty. The meal would be a simple one of grilled kielbasa, with her mom's homemade pierogies, butternut squash soup and a cranberry-pecan salad.

"Yeah." More racket caught her attention as the string quartet arrived and set up, compliments of her brother Darren and his wife, Bree.

Her brother Matthew and his wife, Annie, had delivered the chocolate wedding cake, made by a local bakery. They milled in the kitchen with Cam and his wife, Rose.

Her throat grew tight, knowing her whole family had pitched in to make this day special. She dashed upstairs to dress and peeked at Opal in her crib, sleeping. She caressed her daughter's face. "Tomorrow, we'll wake up at your daddy's house."

Cat had already moved in her things, along with a

Christmas gift for Simon safely tucked under their tree. She'd ordered a hand-carved piece of reclaimed wood that read Home of the Roberts Family. Opal's birth certificate was being changed, as well.

"Cat, you'd better hurry up." Monica stood in the doorway, wearing a simple long-sleeved red dress as her maid of honor.

Cat smiled. "You look gorgeous."

"Thanks. Now, what can I do to help you along? You're going to be late to your own wedding that's only a few feet away."

Cat laughed. "I've got this. Go make sure Zach is here with the rings."

Her oldest brother was standing up with Simon. The rest of her family were here too. She could hear Luke's stereo playing down the hall. Erin had arranged Cat's hair into a fancy swirl and doused it with enough hairspray to keep it in place through a hurricane. Her brothers Ben and Marcus had plowed the driveway, along with a place on the lawn for everyone to park. Everything was ready.

But her.

After brushing her teeth again and freshening her makeup, Cat dropped her sweats in a pile. She reached for the winter-white dress she'd found at the last minute in a boutique store downtown. Made of a heavy silk crepe, it had long sleeves and a slightly draped neckline.

Slipping the dress over her head, she sighed at the luxurious feel of the fabric as the hem brushed her ankles. Cat stepped into light tan pumps and then reached for her bundle of white poinsettias and red roses and looked in the mirror.

Every anniversary going forward, she'd remember this Christmas as the one when joy became real. This newly found joy was not some tinsel-based hope that got tossed out with the Christmas tree either. This joy would last because God was real to her in a very new sense and He'd never forsake her.

Her opal engagement ring flashed with color and she smiled. She wore no other jewelry. Nothing compared to the ring Simon had made from a hunk of rock that had brought them together. Simon would be with her too, by her side for better or worse, and Cat finally believed in *for better.*

A knock at the door brought her mother inside. "Oh, Cat, you look beautiful."

She rushed to give her mother a kiss. "Thank you for being an example I can follow."

Her mom's eyes teared up. "I'm so proud of who you've become."

"I've got a big job now as a mom." Cat's eyes filled too.

"You're a good one, Cat." Her mother patted her arm. "Speaking of which, Opal is waking up. I'll change her and then meet you downstairs."

Cat watched her mom lift Opal out of the swaddled blanket to reveal a red velvet romper. Her little holiday baby was in for the best Christmas present ever—a complete family.

Another knock at the door and her father stepped in. "Everyone's here. Ready?"

She smiled at her parents. She'd put them through a lot and yet they'd never stopped believing in her. "I am."

Taking her father's hand, she walked out of her old room, down the stairs and into the warmth of everyone gathered for this moment.

Simon stood, waiting, looking dapper in his dark suit. He looked up and smiled, his dark eyes never leaving hers.

She kept her gaze locked on his as she approached,

breaking contact only to accept a kiss from her father before he offered her hand to Simon.

Intertwining her fingers with his, Cat knew the instant connection she'd felt the moment they'd met hadn't been wrong. God had brought them back together for a reason. He'd had forever in mind for them.

Simon leaned close. "I've never been happier."

She nodded. "I know. Me too."

Their painful pasts would always be part of who they were. Those pasts had shaped them, but neither would define them. With God's grace, they could move forward and meet new adventures together, with joy.

* * * * *

Pick up these other stories in
Jenna Mindel's Maple Springs series:

Falling for the Mom-to-Be
A Soldier's Valentine
A Temporary Courtship
An Unexpected Family

Available now from Love Inspired!

Find more great reads at www.LoveInspired.com

Dear Reader,

Thank you so much for reading my last book in the Maple Springs series. I hope you've enjoyed Cat and Simon's journey to self-forgiveness, peace and finally love.

This was my most difficult book to bring together. For quite some time, I struggled with Cat's character. I didn't understand the depths of her pain until I researched online stories of people who'd caused an accidental death. I was deeply moved and I hope I've touched this subject with compassion. There is no pat answer to soothe such grief, but I do believe in a big God with the power to heal. If we let Him.

As I wrap up my visits with the Zelinsky family during my favorite time of the year, my prayer for this Christmas season is that we'd draw closer to God with grateful hearts that are full of His love for others.

My warmest wishes to you for a very Merry Christmas and joyful New Year.

Jenna

I love to hear from readers. Please visit my website at www.jennamindel.com or follow me on www.Facebook.com/authorjennamindel or drop me a note c/o Love Inspired Books, 195 Broadway, 24th floor, New York, NY 10007.

COMING NEXT MONTH FROM
Love Inspired®

Available November 20, 2018

AMISH CHRISTMAS MEMORIES
Indiana Amish Brides • by Vannetta Chapman
While mending a fence on his farm, Caleb Wittmer discovers an Amish woman stumbling down the snowy road with no coat, no *kapp*—and no memory. Now he has one Christmas goal: help her remember her past so he can return to his uncomplicated life...but his heart has other plans.

HER AMISH CHRISTMAS GIFT
Women of Lancaster County • by Rebecca Kertz
When Nathaniel Peachy's brother is injured while his family is away, he must accept help on the farm from Charlotte Stoltzfus. But as they work together, can Charlie prove that she's no longer the troublesome girl he remembers, but instead a grown woman worthy of love?

A COWBOY CHRISTMAS
by Linda Goodnight and Ruth Logan Herne
Spend Christmas with two handsome cowboys in these brand-new holiday novellas, where a bachelor is reunited with the only woman he ever considered marrying, and a single mom and a widowed minister find love, healing and an instant family.

THE RANCHER'S CHRISTMAS MATCH
Mercy Ranch • by Brenda Minton
Single mom Rebecca Martin wants a fresh start with her little girl, so when she hears that a philanthropist in Oklahoma is offering buildings rent-free for a year, it's the perfect opportunity. Falling in love isn't part of the bargain...but with ex-soldier Isaac West, it's hard to resist.

A CHRISTMAS BABY FOR THE COWBOY
Cowboy Country • by Deb Kastner
With help from Alyssa Emerson, his late best friend's little sister, Cash Coble steps up to be a daddy to his baby daughter. But as much as he's drawn to Alyssa, he can't allow himself to love her...because he has a secret that could push her away for good.

MISTLETOE TWINS
Rocky Mountain Haven • by Lois Richer
Returning home to foster the twins she hopes to adopt, Adele Parker partners with her childhood friend, former military pilot Mac McDowell, to start a trail-riding program. And the more time she spends with the injured cowboy, the more she believes he'd make the perfect husband and daddy.

LICNM1118

Get 4 FREE REWARDS!

We'll send you 2 FREE Books
<u>plus</u> 2 FREE Mystery Gifts.

Love Inspired® books feature contemporary inspirational romances with Christian characters facing the challenges of life and love.

FREE
Value Over
$20

SPECIAL EXCERPT FROM

When a young Amish woman has amnesia during the holidays, will a handsome Amish farmer help her regain her memories?

Read on for a sneak preview of
Amish Christmas Memories *by Vannetta Chapman, available December 2018 from Love Inspired.*

"What's your name?"

The woman's eyes widened and her hand shook so that she could barely hold the mug of tea without spilling it. She set it carefully on the coffee table. "I don't—I don't know my name."

"How can you not know your own name?" Caleb asked. "Do you know where you live?"

"Nein."

"What were you doing out there?"

"Out where?"

"Where was your coat and your *kapp*?"

"Caleb, now's not the time to interrogate the poor girl." His *mamm* stood and moved beside her on the couch. She picked up the small book of poetry. "You were carrying this, when Caleb found you. Do you remember it?"

"I don't. This was mine?"

"Found it in the snow," Caleb said. "Right beside where you collapsed."

"So it must be mine."

Caleb noticed that the woman's hands trembled as she opened the cover and stared down at the first page. With one finger, she traced the handwriting there.

LIEXP1118

"Rachel. I think my name is Rachel."

Rachel let her fingers brush over the word again and again. Rachel. Yes, that was her name. She was sure of it. She remembered writing it in the front of the book—she'd used a pen that her *mamm* had given her. She could almost picture herself, somewhere else. She could almost see her mother.

"My *mamm* gave me the pen and the book…for my birthday, I think. I wrote my name—wrote it right here."

"Your *mamm*. So you remember her?"

"Praise be to *Gotte*," Caleb's *dat* said, a smile spreading across his face.

"Is there someone we can call? If you remember the name of your bishop…" Caleb had sat down in the rocker his mother had vacated and was staring at her intensely.

They all were.

She closed her eyes, hoping to feel the memory again. She tried to see the room or the house or the people, but the memory had receded as quickly as it had come, leaving her with a pulsing headache.

She struggled to keep the feelings of panic at bay. Her heart was hammering, and her hands were shaking, and she could barely make sense of the questions they were pelting at her.

Who were these people?

Where was she?

Who was she?

She needed to remember what had happened.

She needed to go home.

Don't miss
Amish Christmas Memories *by Vannetta Chapman,*
available December 2018 wherever
Love Inspired® *books and ebooks are sold.*

www.LoveInspired.com

LIEXP1118

Looking for inspiration in tales
of hope, faith and heartfelt romance?

Check out **Love Inspired**® and
Love Inspired® **Suspense** books!

New books available every month!

CONNECT WITH US AT:

Facebook.com/groups/HarlequinConnection

 Facebook.com/HarlequinBooks

 Twitter.com/HarlequinBooks

 Instagram.com/HarlequinBooks

 Pinterest.com/HarlequinBooks

ReaderService.com

Love Inspired.

LIGENRE2018R2

Toby Potter watched the flames shoot toward the sky as he raced toward the building. "Robin!"

Sirens screamed closer. Toby had been on his way home when he'd spotted Robin's car in the parking lot of the lab. Ever since Robin had discovered his deception—orders to get close to her and figure out what was going on in the lab—she'd kept him at arm's length, her narrow-eyed stare hot enough to singe his eyebrows if he dare try to get too close.

Tonight, he'd planned to apologize profusely—again—and ask if there was anything he could do to earn her trust back. Only to pull into the parking lot, be greeted by the loud boom and watch flames shoot out of the window near the front door.

Heart pounding, Toby scanned the front door and rushed forward only to be forced back by the intense heat. Smoke billowed toward the dark night sky while the fire grew hotter and bigger. Mini explosions followed. Chemicals.

"Robin!"

Toby jumped into his truck and drove around to the back only to find it not much better, although it did seem to be more smoke than flames. Robin was in that building, and he was afraid he'd failed to protect her. Big-time.

Toby parked near the tree line in case more explosions were coming.

At the back door, he grasped the handle and pulled. Locked. Of course. Using both fists, he pounded on the glass-and-metal door. "Robin!"

Another explosion from inside rocked Toby back, but he was able to keep his feet under him. He figured the blast was on the other end of the building—where he knew Robin's station was. If she was anywhere near that station, there was no way she was still alive. "No, please no," he whispered. No one was around to hear him, but maybe God was listening.

Don't miss
Holiday Amnesia *by Lynette Eason,*
available December 2018 wherever
Love Inspired® Suspense books and ebooks are sold.

www.LoveInspired.com

LISEXP1118

Love Inspired®

Inspirational Romance to Warm Your Heart and Soul

Join our social communities to connect with other readers who share your love!

Sign up for the Love Inspired newsletter at **www.LoveInspired.com** to be the first to find out about upcoming titles, special promotions and exclusive content.

CONNECT WITH US AT:

Facebook.com/groups/HarlequinConnection

 Facebook.com/LoveInspiredBooks

 Twitter.com/LoveInspiredBks

LISOCIAL2018